Other Books by
Jess E. Owen

Song of the Summer King

Skyfire

A Shard of Sun

By the Silver Wind

Jess E. Owen

The Starward Light
and other tales

five elements press

Copyright © 2017 by Jess E. Owen
ALL RIGHTS RESERVED. No part of this publication may be reproduced, distributed, or transmitted in any form or by any means, including photocopying, recording, or other electronic or mechanical methods, without the prior written permission of the publisher, except in the case of brief quotations embodied in critical reviews and certain other noncommercial uses permitted by copyright law. For permission requests, write to the publisher, addressed "Attention: Permissions Coordinator," at the address below.
Five Elements Press
Suite 305
500 Depot Street
Whitefish, MT 59937
www.fiveelementspress.com

PUBLISHER'S NOTE
This is a work of fiction. Any references to historical events, real people, or real locales are used fictitiously. Other names, characters, places, or incidents are the product of the author's imagination, and any resemblance to actual events, locales, or persons, living or dead, are purely coincidental.

Cover art by Jennifer Miller © 2017
Cover layout, typography, and interior formatting by Terry Roy
Author photo by Jessica Lowry

ISBN-13: 978-0-9967676-5-1

First Paperback Edition

Contents

The Starward Light 1
Beneath the Windward Sun 81
The Salmon Run 141
About the Author 187

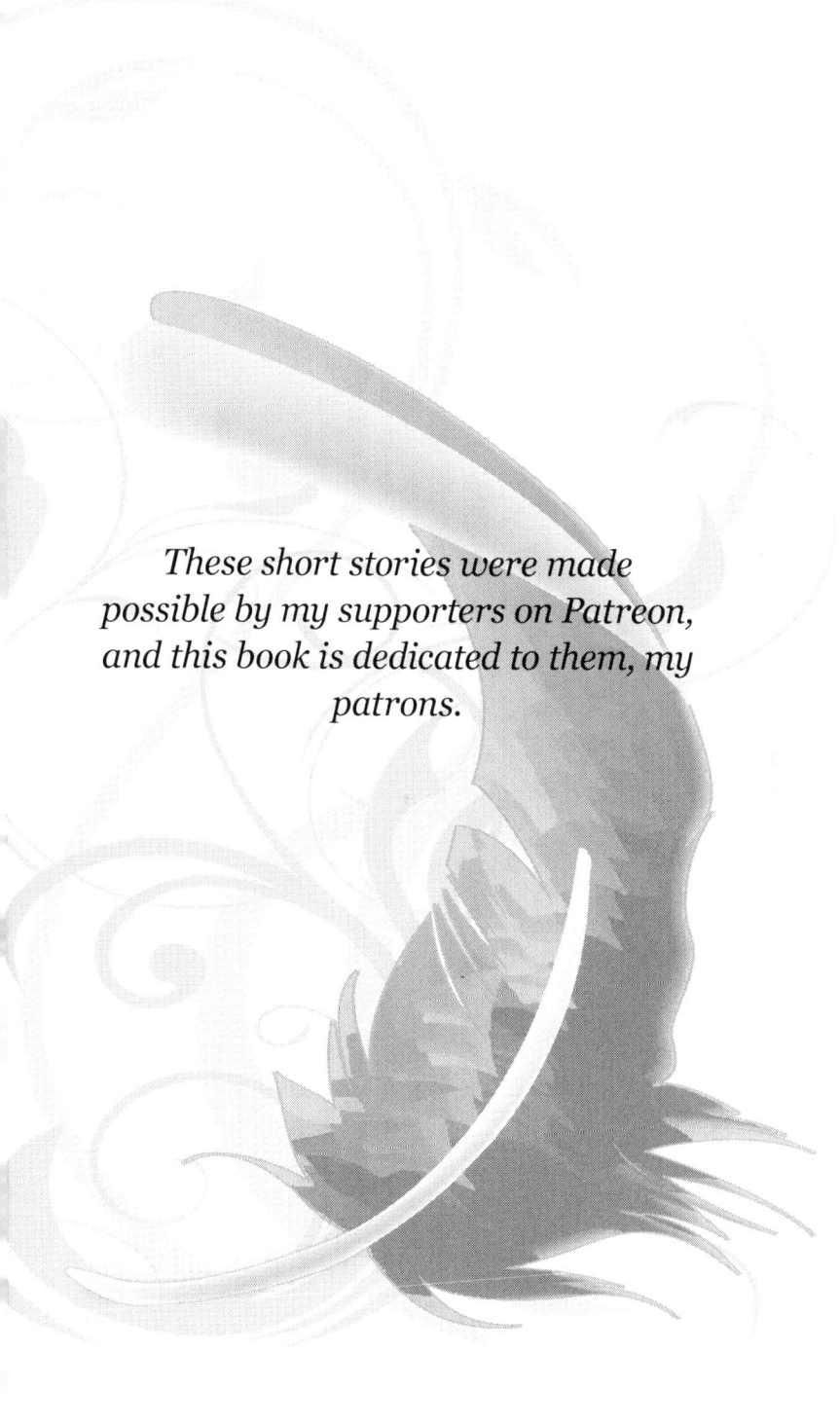

These short stories were made possible by my supporters on Patreon, and this book is dedicated to them, my patrons.

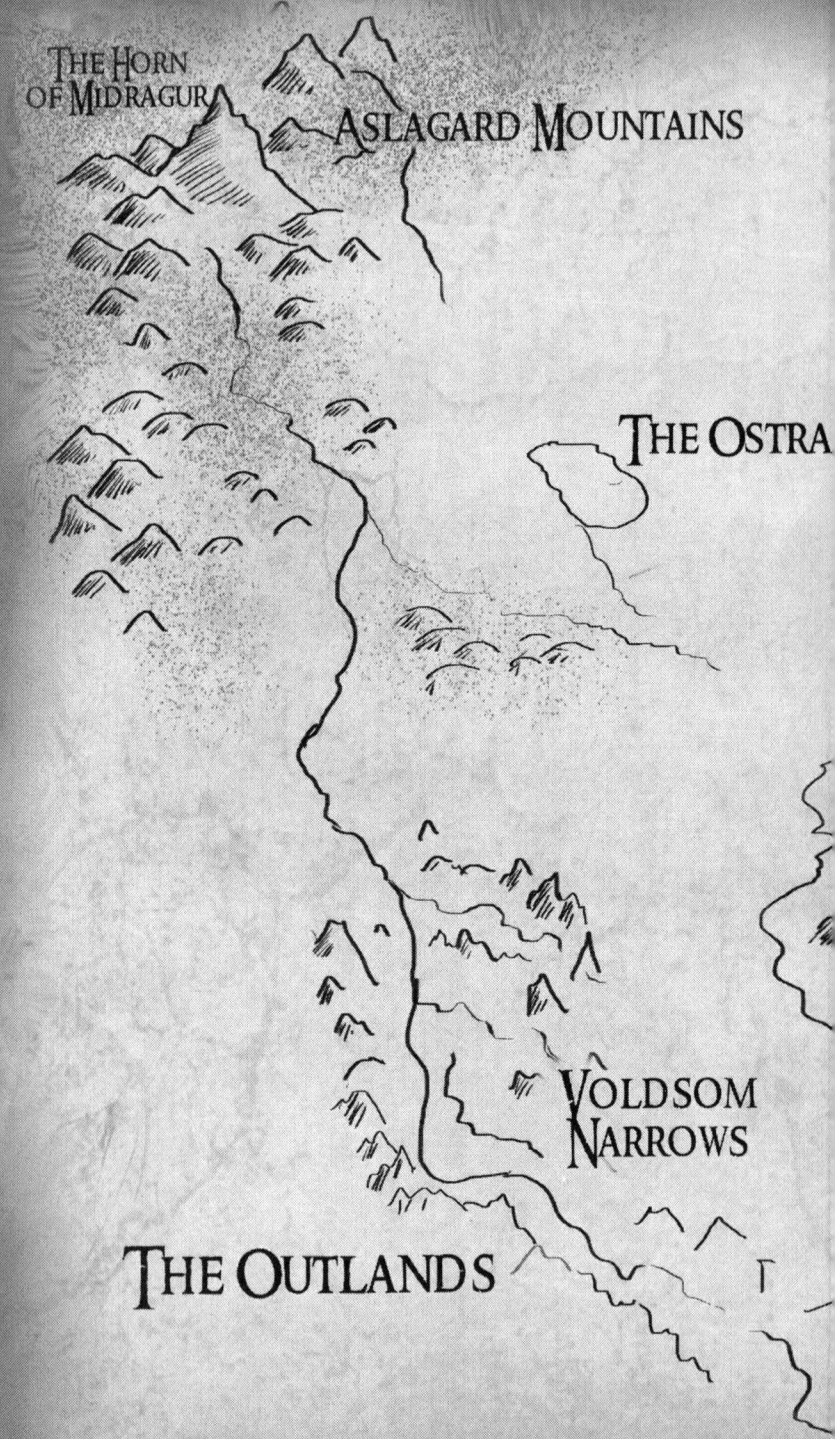

HORES # THE WINDEROST

DAWN SPIRE

THE DAWN REACH

THE VANHEIM SHORE

A gryfon's view of
The Silver Isles

Starward
Nightward
Dawnward
Windward

Pebble's Throw

Talon's Reach

Star Isle

Crow Wing

The gryfon colony of Windwater

Sun Isle

The White Mountains

Black Rock

The Nightrun River

The Nesting Cliffs

The Windward Sea

THE STARWARD LIGHT

A Tale of the Silver Isles

Jess E. Owen

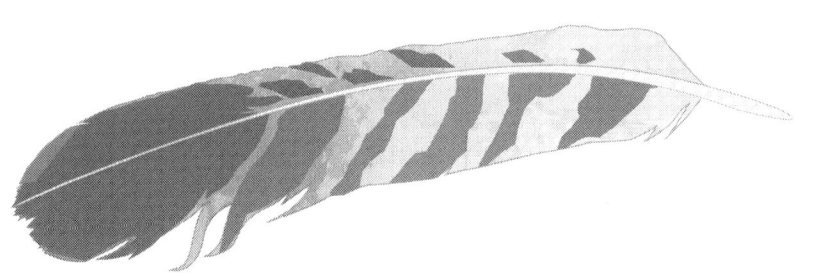

CRYSTALLINE SPECKS OF SNOW FLURRIED across the white plain that swept away from the gryfon nesting cliffs. White sparkles swirled and dusted the wings of the plump gryfesses who trudged out of the birch woods and along a well-packed trail that led, in the shortest possible course, from the river to the cliffs that overlooked the crashing sea.

Second in line, Brynja, daughter-of-Mar, kept a lookout to either side. Though any attacks were unlikely, she had learned to expect the unlikely.

A lone warrior circled above the line, keeping a wary eye. He was mottled gray flashing iridescent lavender in the sun, with a falcon mask and the unmistakably strong, yet sleek build of a half-blood Aesir.

"Tollak!" Sigrun called to him, walking just ahead of Brynja. The pride's healer was smaller, slim, and plain dove-brown, and led the line of pregnant gryfesses in their daily trek. Though there were few, if any, enemies left in their isles, no one was willing to drop their guard after the last, brutal year of fighting and fear. "Send word ahead to Pala and Idunn to ready some chamomile for the queen."

Tollak cried an affirmative, glad for the task—anything for the healers. He hadn't chosen a mate on the Daynight, but he watched and fretted over each pregnant gryfess as if they were his own.

"I'm fine," Brynja grumbled, knowing they saw not the huntress who had helped Shard in the Winderost, but only a sturdy, ruddy, round gryfess plodding along like the rest.

"So fine you won't slow down," Sigrun said over her wing, casting a critical eye over her—the youngest queen, Sigrun had told her, that the Isles had known in some time.

Brynja once heard her own mother boast that she was as comely and strong as a gryfess might be, blessed by Tor with a mind sharper than her talons, and a heart as warm as her russet feathers. She got her golden eyes from the line of En, and hadn't yet met a gryfon with the same splash of red flecks on pale cheek feathers, such as she had.

Sigrun was still studying her, and Brynja wondered what the healer was thinking. Then she knew, for Sigrun told her, "You should rest more as the days get colder. Shard's heir sits heavy."

"Forming big dreams, no doubt," Brynja said, unable to keep the spark of pride from her voice. Sigrun looked indulgent—no doubt she'd seen many pregnant gryfesses dreaming big dreams for their kits over the years.

"Or big wings," remarked Dagny, the gryfess who insisted on walking alongside Brynja, which meant she must plow through belly-deep snow. "I'm certain it will be a female, a huntress with your strength and his skill in the air."

Dagny's rich brown feathers reminded Brynja of the earth after a rain, but she brushed the thought aside. It was much too early to yearn for spring. She was very glad Dagny had decided to remain through the winter, when most of the Aesir had flown home after the Daynight earlier in the summer. She couldn't imagine the birth of her first kit without her wingsister at her side.

"I'll be happy either way," Brynja said. "Male or female. It will be Shard's and mine."

They ruminated on about the possibilities for Brynja and Shard's kit, and Brynja allowed herself a happy ruffle of her wing feathers.

Behind Brynja, other gryfesses murmured their own excitement and hopes for their kits. They were a small band, only seven that year, for they had suffered many losses. Some gryfesses who might have mated had lost their beloved, and still mourned. The Vanir who had returned to the Silver Isles after ten years of exile were still learning who they were, and the Aesir and half-bloods who lived there all those ten years allowed them space to do so. Though hope and peace were so far the trademarks of Shard's reign, the Daynight had still seen fewer matings than previous years.

When Brynja glanced again at the sky, searching for Tollak, she saw instead a slender, pale form gliding toward them to land. Ragna, the delicate color of a winter cloud, or the palest color of foam on the sea, landed neatly a single leap from the line before bounding forward through the snow.

The Widow Queen's eyes matched her son's, the pale green of summer moss. Brynja envied the Vanir and half-blood's long winter feather and fluffy layer of down. She hoped her kit would be blessed with the extra protection as well.

"How is everyone?" Ragna called to the line of gryfesses. Respectful assurances greeted her question. Two gryfesses Ragna's age, Maja and Ketil, called to her from the middle of the line. The wingsisters were too old to bear kits, but helped the gryfesses all the same. They also mantled to Ragna, and Brynja noticed, trying not to take offense, for she herself showed Shard's mother respect every chance she could. Brynja knew the old Vanir acknowledged Brynja as their queen, but Brynja still wasn't sure how well they loved her.

"My lady . . ." Ragna began, approaching Brynja.

Sigrun lifted a forefoot to make Ragna pause—the only gryfon in the pride who would dare to interrupt her, for she was a healer, and they were wingsisters after all. "Unless you're here with simple well-wishes,

I must insist that you not press Brynja with anymore worries or duties right now."

"Oh, do press me," Brynja said, ears perking toward the pale, older queen. Sigrun eyed her sideways, and Brynja tried to ignore her. She must prove herself as a worthy queen of the Vanir, and a little weariness wouldn't stop her.

Ragna looked between them, and appeared to take Brynja's order over Sigrun's. "Have you considered what celebrations we'll hold during the Long Night?"

Dagny's ears perked up and she raised her wings. "Oh, is there feasting? In the Winderost, we have the Wild Hunt—"

"So you've told us," Ragna murmured. "But it won't do, here."

Dagny's ears flicked back and she looked to Brynja, crestfallen, her long, feathered tail drooping to drag in the snow.

"I know little of the way the Vanir observe the Long Night here," Brynja said carefully. She couldn't believe the Vanir still considered it autumn, with snow on the ground and bitter cold nights and short days. But until the Long Night set, they did. "Shard, of course, hasn't been able to tell me either." Shard, who had grown up under the Aesir conquerors, who didn't yet know all the traditions of his own ancestors.

"There hasn't been time," Sigrun said, as if to reassure her. "We'll get it all sorted." She watched Brynja closely, appearing to search for signs of stress. Brynja wasn't worried. Many a kit had been whelped that spring after a year of extreme duress, and all were healthy. So far as she knew, anyway—those kits whose parents had remained in the Silver Isles.

For a moment it was silent as Ragna and Sigrun probably thought on the Long Night "tradition" of the Aesir conquerors: cowering in the dark until the sun rose again. Brynja knew it would not do, this year, but the Vanir had not yet told her what they expected of her, if anything.

Apparently, she was about to find out.

"We will tell you all you need to know." Ragna turned to walk with them, just behind Brynja along the trail, to show deference, she thought, and felt grateful. "The question is whether all observances will be made, with the mixed pride."

"The Vanir haven't been allowed a proper Long Night in ten years," Sigrun said. "Why, by Tyr's left wing, would we not want to do all of it? Shard is Vanir, after all."

Brynja tried not to laugh, for Sigrun sounded so much like her gruff mate, Caj. When Ragna and Brynja merely looked at her quietly, she appeared to understand. The entire pride was not made up of Vanir, but many half-bloods, many exiles, and several Aesir, like Caj, who had come as conquerors but stayed as family even when many chose to return to their homeland. Brynja tried to imagine any gryfon pressing Caj into a moonlight observance, or a starlit flight, or anything involving the dark, strange Vanir traditions, or anything else he might not want to do, and ruffled her feathers uncomfortably. She knew the stubborn souls of Aesir well enough to know that none of them would be happy feeling cut out by a purely Vanir celebration, and the Vanir would certainly be hurt by being ignored, here on their first chance to hold a celebration that was really theirs.

Ragna and Sigrun were watching her. Dagny glanced uncomfortably over her shoulder at Ketil, Maja, and the half-bloods, then pressed closer to Brynja, offering warmth and reassurance.

Brynja soaked it up, gladly, and was able to speak. "I think it best," she began slowly, her gaze sliding between Ragna and Sigrun, "to bring the matter to Shard. He knows the pride best, and he is Vanir. He will make wise and thoughtful decisions befitting the mixed pride."

Ragna exchanged a look with Sigrun, ducked her head respectfully, then lifted it, watching Brynja sternly. "We will speak to

Shard regarding his preferences. But you should know that we consider Long Night to be Tor's time. She, the huntress, who guides us, and who brings the thunder, and lights our wings in the dark. It is appropriate, my lady, for *you,* as queen, as Tor's talons on earth, to have the final say. Summer is over. Winter, and night, are Tor's time."

Brynja tilted her head, blinking at the blunt statement, then looked to Sigrun, who nodded once. For a moment, Brynja's heart glowed. What an honor, to oversee such an event!

Then cold uncertainty stole over heart. What would all those Vanir think about their most sacred time of the season being overseen, not by one of their own, but by an Aesir, a windlander whose own kin had conquered the Isles they had just reclaimed?

Dagny made a soft, uncomfortable sound, looking between Ragna and Sigrun.

Brynja met their eyes, clearly saw the doubt they shared, and raised her head. "Tell me what I need to know. I promise we will make this a Long Night to remember."

A DOZEN FLEDGES GLEEFULLY dragged fragrant evergreen boughs from the field toward the cliffs, even as Brynja spied Tollak and others flying in from Star Island with more, their talons bursting with prickly branches of fir, spruce, and boughs from the slender, long-trunk pines.

Fledglings with more advanced flying skills had joined the warriors, filling their talons not with pine, but with what red rowan berries could be found in the winter forests. Ragna hadn't yet told Brynja their purpose or meaning, saying only that they were for the Third Night.

Brynja directed those with pine boughs toward the dens of the pregnant gryfesses and the bachelor males, whose nests were to be adorned by the branches for the duration of the Long Night. Ketil and Maja stood near, helping to answer questions and explain to the fledges that the branches were to remind the gryfesses of the life they carried, and the bachelors of summer and life and warm times to come, and their duties to the pride.

"In two days the sun will set," Ragna instructed. A teal-tipped, gray half-blood fledge bounded past, bearing a spruce branch she had caused to sparkled by decorating it with crystallized sea salt. "That's lovely, Mist!" Ragna called.

Brynja nodded once, drawing Ragna's attention back to her. "Two days. Will that be enough time for all the preparations, with the days so short?" The sun hovered low on the horizon, leaving only three marks of light each day now. Brynja had never seen such short days, and still couldn't imagine the Long Night, when the sun wouldn't rise at all. "We might have to sacrifice a few—"

"Never fear," said Ketil briskly, from her left. Brynja managed to keep her neck feathers smooth. Shard had found the Vanir gryfess and her daughter, Keta, in the Outlands of the Winderost. Brynja knew that the older huntress had hoped Shard might fall in love with her own daughter, but Shard had pledged his heart to Brynja long before. Much had mended between them after they reclaimed the Isles, and over the spring and summer, but tension crackled about the Vanir now as Brynja prepared for *their* festivities.

"Maja and I have been preparing," Ketil went on when Ragna and Brynja both looked at her. "Of course," she said coolly, "we had assumed you would honor the traditions of the Vanir that were ignored and suppressed these long years, so we looked ahead to what would be needed."

"Of course," Brynja echoed quietly. She dared not look to Ragna for shelter from Ketil's cold voice. She was certain the Widow Queen shared a quiet disappointment that her son did not mate with a Vanir, even if she hid it better. "What have you done so far?"

"We've fermented fruits for the Second Night," Maja said, stepping forward. The gryfess was pale, but with a subtle and attractive yellow cast to her feathers, like a finch or prairie lark. She was the mother of Halvden, a half-blood who had chosen, with his mate, to take their kit to the Winderost and live under Kjorn's rule. Her Aesir mate had been killed by wolves two summers ago, and Brynja gathered he was not much missed by anyone in the pride. She denned now with Ketil and Keta, and didn't seem to miss any of her own absent kin.

"And gathered salt for the fishing," Ketil said. The middle-aged wingsisters went on proudly, if not a hair smugly, about their preparations for the Long Night. Brynja wanted to feel only gratitude and relief, but their haughtiness and surety wore on her, and she could only nod, making a mental tally.

Another fledge darted past with a sweet-smelling branch, laughing, and that eased Brynja's mood somewhat. Enough that she was able to dip her head in genuine thanks when Ketil finished describing all the work they had done. "Then we'll be able to observe all your celebrations properly." She drew a slow, calming breath, and felt her kit shift in her belly.

She must've winced, for Maja eyed her sharply. "Do you need to rest, my lady?"

Brynja fluffed her wings. *Rest, indeed, and let all of you do the preparations well shed of me, saying I didn't care enough to bother . . .* "Oh, no. Shard's little one is anxious to get flying, is all."

"No doubt." Ragna's voice warmed considerably, as Brynja thought it might at the mention of her son's heir.

"So now that I know we'll have the expected foods, tell me the days," Brynja said. "And thank you again, Maja and Ketil. You honor yourselves and the pride with your forethought and work."

Surprise flickered in their faces and, to Brynja's pleasure, both mantled and murmured thanks.

"There are twelve days of the Long Night," Ragna said, and Brynja tried to grasp the idea of days of darkness, and nights of darkness, and how they would measure the time. Shard had seemed excited to show her the turning of the stars and had almost convinced her that it would actually be quite easy to tell when the next "day" began, so she'd hid her unease from him.

"The first sunset is the Mother's Night," Ragna explained, "when we feast and we each choose a huntress ancestor or mentor to honor—one who is now passed to the Sunlit Land. We name them under the moon and thank them for whatever sacrifices they made that gave us our lives here."

Brynja nodded. The first ancestor who came to mind was En, the beginning of the line which branched and ended not only in

Sverin and Kjorn, but herself. "Very good. And we eat fish?"

"Of course," Ketil said, sounding surprised, as if to ask, *what else?*

"I didn't know if special hunting provisions might be made," Brynja said quietly, glancing to her.

"No," Ketil said firmly. "We have never eaten red meat on the Long Night."

Brynja thought of the Wild Hunt in the Winderost, the grand feast, the fires that were a new tradition within the last nine years. "What of fires?"

Maja and Ketil looked scandalized. Their ears slicked back, their eyes widened, then narrowed, and feathers fluffed up indignantly. Brynja looked quickly to Ragna, alarmed that she'd offended them so quickly.

Ragna brushed her talons idly through the snow. "The Long Night is Tor's time. We honor the darkness, and the winter in which the earth rests and readies for spring, as a pregnant gryfess rests and readies for new life."

"I see." Brynja began to walk again, fighting a cramp that had formed near her ribs from wherever her kit had chosen to settle. She chose her words carefully. "I do want to honor the traditions of the Vanir. But we are a mixed pride, and we should all be acknowledged. In the Winderost, we enjoy fires to keep out the winter cold, and I believe that will be a new pleasure to everyone here."

Ketil bristled and stepped forward, though she did lower her head a degree to show a small measure of deference. "With utmost respect I must disagree. My lady, the Aesir have had their way on these isles for the last ten—"

"Have they?" Brynja asked, looking from Ketil to Ragna. "It was my understanding they also cowered and fasted in the dark right alongside the Vanir, and slept, and waited long, uneasy nights for the dawn. That does *not* sound like the traditions of the Aesir I know."

Silence stretched between them as Ketil's ears laid back. Ragna broke it, looking away toward the icy sea. "That is true. Sverin's fear of the darkness and his nightmare of the wyrms prevented any of us from acknowledging change of season properly."

"My lady," Ketil said, looking betrayed.

"We will observe traditions of the Vanir," Brynja said firmly, "*and* the Aesir who have also lived unhappy days in the dark. We will help them overcome the last ten years of fear, learn to celebrate Tor's time, and fly a new wind of celebration."

"What did you have in mind?" Maja asked, and Ketil offered her a skeptical look as well.

"A feast, as well," Brynja said. "On the Second Night." When the other gryfesses would have argued, she lifted her wings. "Shard has allies on other isles who may grant us rights to hunt red meat, or birds, or the like. You've told me that aside from the Daynight, the Vanir treasured this time of year above all others. I hope, when we're done, the entire pride will feel the same. Now," she looked again at Ragna, "Tell me of the other eleven nights. But let's walk," she said, wincing at demanding kick from her kit.

"Very well," said Ragna, and Brynja could not read her still, regal face.

"If you need more help do let us know," Ketil said, but challenge edged her voice, and Brynja did her best not to bristle. *I'm not a brittle twig, about to snap in the cold. I'll show them I can do this, and I will make Shard proud.*

"Thank you," she said, as smoothly as she could manage. "I'm sure I can handle it from here." She looked to Ragna, and tilted her head. "My lady?"

Ragna nodded, and they walked, and she explained the twelve days of the Long Night.

The Second Night is the time of songs and indulgence. The grown warriors and huntresses not bearing kits may eat the fermented fruits, and we feast. We sing the winter songs, and teach them to the youngest fledges. You will want a good voice to lead us.

Brynja scoured the pride for their knowledge of who had the finest voice, and one name came above the rest: Astri, daughter-of-Ollar. Brynja didn't remember her singing at all over the spring or even at the exuberant Daynight and Halfnight celebrations. When she dug deeper, most cautioned that she might not accept the request if Brynja made it. Brynja was too closely related to Sverin, who had killed Astri's mate, and whom she had not yet forgiven despite all the time that had passed.

"Let me speak with her," said Dagr, Astri's brother-by-mate. Brynja stood with him at the edge of the birch woods, where more bachelor males gathered wood for the fires she still planned to have for the twelve cold nights of celebration. "Let me talk to her before you do, my queen."

Brynja shifted her feet in the snow, seeking solid ground, but only packed ice and snow met her talons. "That seems cowardly . . ."

Dagr, slender but strapping with handsome feathers that glinted copper against the snow, shook his head. "Let me? The Vanir call it 'breaking the ice.' She still has a . . . a shield of ice about her. I'll speak to her of the celebrations and mention the night of singing. I know she'll be excited to honor the traditions of our Vanir ancestors. Then, she might be more open to hearing from you."

Brynja considered him, the warrior whose father was once exiled, who had defied Sverin by flying to find exiled Vanir, returned again to find his younger brother dead, fought the wyrms, and chose to live in Shard's mixed pride . . . if there were any she trusted to be forthright, it was him. "Thank you. I accept." She glanced to the low, weak sun. "We don't have much time."

"I'll speak to her when she returns from fishing."

Brynja nodded once. Tollak approached from the woods then, mantled briefly to Brynja, and stepped up to Dagr with the closeness of a wingbrother. He paused, giving Brynja a quick look up and down. "My lady, are you well?"

Brynja lifted her head higher, wondering if she looked weary. She felt warm, but healthy. "Just fine. The exercise is good. Thank you."

One ear ticked back skeptically, but Dagr nudged him with a wing and they began to discuss the wood stores rather than continue to stare at her.

Brynja turned from them her next task, running through all Ragna had told her.

The Third Night, we honor the dead who have passed during the year. You will need one to speak for those who died of natural ways, and those who died in battle.

Brynja went for the easy one first, and found Caj afield with the fledges, overseeing their spars in the snow.

"My lady!" he called, when he saw Brynja trudging forward through the snow. "Stop, I'll come to you." He leaped forward, bounding until he jumped into the sky, and flew the distance between them to save her the trouble. It was good to see him flying again, after having first met him when he had a broken wing.

She longed to fly but felt too heavy. Her own muscles had warmed from all the walking around, though they quivered slightly. Sigrun had warned her against overexertion, but Brynja couldn't imagine such a thing. Her female forebears had carried and whelped kits for generations before her, and surely they didn't sit around eating and watching the sun rise and set from their nests all day. She had a celebration to plan.

"Caj," she said as he landed before her, and wondered if she sounded too relieved at not having to walk any further. Thinking of Sigrun's warnings, she sat down to rest, knowing he wouldn't be offended. "I have something to ask of you."

"Anything within my power to give," he rumbled, folding his broad, cobalt wings.

Perhaps it was a mistake to ask an Aesir when the tradition was of the Vanir—but then, who better? Caj had chosen the Silver Isles over returning to his homeland, even though his own daughter ruled as queen of the Dawn Spire there now. He was a warrior, respected, advising the King's Guard Sverin had created and Shard had kept intact, and overseeing the warrior training of all the fledglings in the pride. Who better?

"We are preparing to observe the Long Night as the Vanir have done in days past. One of the nights is devoted to honoring those who fell in battle during the last year." She paused, and knew they were both thinking of his wingbrother, Sverin, the Red King, and all the rest who had fallen to the claws of the wyrms that spring. "I was hoping you would speak for them."

"A Vanir tradition?" His hard, pale yellow eyes flickered with surprise, and he looked across the snowy plain toward the sea. Clouds pressed low, dimming the light, and Brynja thought of all that was left to do.

Everyone had offered help—Shard, Dagny, Ragna, the half-bloods who fully honored her as their queen—but these were things she wanted to do on her own. She would show Ketil, Maja, and any others who doubted her sincerity that she could rule the mixed pride well, honoring Tor, honoring all. And she could do it alone, as she was meant to.

"Say you will," she urged Caj. "You've chosen a life here. Show them we honor the Vanir traditions by partaking in them."

He made a gruff noise, eyed her plump form and, she thought, probably considered what his mate would think if she found out he turned down the honor. Finally, he lowered his head, lifting his wings. "I will. Though I can't promise how well anyone will like it."

"Oh, thank you," she breathed. For a moment she thought of abrasive Ketil, but decided she didn't give two feathers if the gryfess liked her choices or not. "Ragna will tell you all you need to know."

He ducked his head, and as Brynja rose to go asked, "Would you like to stay a bit and see how the fledges are coming along?"

Brynja hesitated. *A well-disguised and tactful attempt to get me to rest longer,* she thought indignantly, and managed not to sweep her tail through the snow. "I wish I could, but we have only a mark of the sun left and I still must arrange the rest of the nights."

For a moment, it looked as if the big, burly old warrior would force her to sit, then he appeared to think better of it and nodded once. "If you need help, my wings and talons are yours."

Touched, Brynja shook herself and smoothed her feathers, trying not to feel so defensive. She knew that Shard sometimes felt uncertain as a Vanir king overseeing Aesir who chose to live under his rule—but still he made confident choices, knowing they had chosen him.

No one had chosen Brynja but Shard. She had to prove herself to them. "Thank you. I will keep that in mind."

Caj watched her with his hard, unreadable eyes. "Do, my lady."

She cast a gaze over the snowy field. "Have you seen any of the elders today?"

"Any in particular?" His eye strayed toward the fledges, who without his stern guidance had dissolved into an aimless, shrieking pile of tumbling snow-covered rumps and wings.

"I was hoping to speak to Frar." She thought of the old, frail Vanir, who had managed to make the long flight from the Outlands in the Winderost to his home, but whose every day, it seemed to Brynja, might be his last. He had no living family, but he was content with Shard as king, and being home. Sometimes it seemed he was waiting for something, clinging to life for one last task. She planned to give him something to do for a little while, anyway.

"I would try the shore, then. Sigrun said he's . . . been speaking to birds quite a lot, of late." Caj offered that news hesitantly, as if it were something to be ashamed of. Brynja wondered at that, for Shard spoke to birds often, though not seabirds. With the exception of a few, he said in general they were only concerned with their next meal and their own pecking order.

"Thank you." She turned, and braced herself for the trek across the snow and down the cliffs to the shore. She felt Caj's eyes on her every step of the way.

By the time she reached the shoreline, her back ached, her neck had tightened and her hind legs, bearing the brunt of her burden, shook like old tree trunks in a hearty wind. The sun touched the horizon, ready to set after only three marks of daylight, and Brynja could have screamed her fury. *How are we meant to have energy to spare for these preparations when we have so little daylight? Or are we meant to prepare in bitter cold darkness, when all I want is to curl up under Shard's wing and sleep?* The thought of another cold fish dinner followed by a dry, bitterly cold night nearly swept the last of her strength from her.

Then she felt the eyes on her. Gryfons sitting atop the cliffs or on the ledges outside their nests near the top had paused speaking, sparring, and decorating with pine boughs and rowan berries to watch her. Brynja realized she stood at the very edge of the cliff, weaving as if dazed, her talons clutching the hard ridge of snow at the precipice.

She forced her ears forward, her back straight, and looked around at the staring eyes. "Has anyone seen Frar?"

"Yes," called Pala from down the cliff. The healer's apprentice was a small, fledging half-blood, her wings and face streaked with a blend of scarlet and striking white. She tended to another pregnant gryfess who appeared to be in the throes of the same cramps Brynja suffered. "Down by the shell-digging rocks. Shall I fetch him to you?"

Brynja bit back a scoff. Fetch an elder who might very well be on his last wing beats to the top of the cliff—indeed, when she was young and strong? "No. Carry on. Thank you."

But the apprentice watched Brynja's entire ungainly, half walking, half sliding trek down the cliff trail, and she felt attention move from her only when she stood safely on the snow of the beach.

Great hunks of ice loomed off shore in the freezing, dazzling sea, creating new temporary obstacles which the Vanir used as watch-posts for fishing. The low, silvery sun lanced through the ice towers and painted them impossible shades of blue and white. The snow that covered the beach was well-packed by gryfon and gull feet, slick with ice here, crunchy and melting with sea salt there, so that Brynja had to watch nearly every step of the way.

Heat pounded through her body, a relief against a rising, frigid wind. Her head felt light, but she carried on toward a place well-known for being rich with mussels. At last she spied old Frar, digging down through the snow to reach the sand and, she supposed, find the mussels and clams the Vanir seemed so fond of on special occasions. The thought of the slick, salty tidbits of meat tightened her belly with nausea and she halted, swallowing hard.

She hoped Shard might've made some progress speaking to the keepers of the herds of the Sun Isle, or the wolves, about red meat for the Second Night celebrations. Since they indulged in fermented fruit and fish eggs and other rich delicacies, red meat or even fowl didn't seem so out of place to Brynja. But no answer had come.

For a moment she stood locked in place, staring at the shadows that gathered on the beach, watching Frar, then the icy waves, pulling in and out.

Her muscles seized against taking another step. She thought of red meat, and how it would offend Ketil, and why she thought it shouldn't.

But what do I know? I'm just an oppressive Aesir, who doesn't respect the traditions . . . lights swam before her eyes, the Wings of the Tor.

The rays of the sun.

They rippled in blinding sheets together, green and gold and shocking rose.

The sun was not setting for the Long Night, and gryfons glared because they knew it was her fault . . . the green became Shard's eyes, disappointed, accusing . . . the sun wasn't setting, and it was all her fault . . .

"My lady!"

A warm head nuzzled her. Brynja twitched, and realized she'd sunk to the snow and closed her eyes, passing into a fevered dream. Fear lanced through her, quick and stabbing. Frar had laid beside her and covered her with a wing, but she was hot, too hot, and she tried to nudge him away, but her tongue stuck to her beak.

When did I last drink water? It couldn't have been the day before . . .

Frar was wise enough to see her distress and moved his wing, but stayed at her side. Through a roaring in her ears, she heard him call for help. For a moment she laid there catching her breath, then, there was the last thing she wanted—fuss and commotion absolutely everywhere.

Pala streaked down from the cliffs, a scarlet and white blur, her talons squeezing around a bundle of herbs, which she stuffed into Brynja's beak without so much as a "by your leave." Behind her came Tollak, Caj, then Ragna, green eyes sparking with worry—or judgment. Brynja couldn't tell . . .

Her head surged with dizziness and she vaguely minded her feet as too many gryfons crowded forward and helped her climb the cliff trail. She managed to croak pathetically, alerting them to her thirst. Firm, gentle talons pressed soaked moss to her beak and she stumbled to a halt. She drank, and more came. They resumed the climb, though she wanted only to curl up on the snow and sleep.

Big males hauled her to her nest, and she couldn't fight them, or refuse help, or admit she needed it. Ashamed, mortified, she collapsed with her back to all of them, drinking in the scent of her own furs and the sweet, warm scent of pine all around.

Blinking back a wave of exhaustion, the last thing Brynja felt was alarm that she hadn't talked to Frar about Third Night, or Astri about singing, and she couldn't remember the tradition of the Twelfth Night . . .

Then she heard Shard's voice, thanking everyone and ordering them out. A familiar, slender wing came around her, and she blinked once, staring blankly at the pine branch near her beak, covered in crystals of salt that glinted like frost in the last light of the last evening.

NIGHTMARES STABBED BRYNJA'S FITFUL sleep. A sun that wouldn't set, burning hot in winter against blinding ice. The kit in her belly felt like a ball of fire, but she was so weary she woke only to suck more water from moss pressed to her beak, and to eat tiny strips of fish that some gryfon—Shard, or Sigrun—fed her, like a kit.

Slips of words came to her. Fever. Overworked. Stressed.

Then, *sunset*. She had to wake for the last sunset . . .

But Shard and Pala gave her fish coated in herbs to make her sleep through the night, and the last hours of daylight slipped through her talons like river water.

When Brynja woke again, it was dark, and she knew the Long Night had begun without her. Disappointment and frustration quickened her heart. She had failed to finish the preparations.

She pushed herself up to a sitting position. "Shard."

Her king was curled up at her side, having slept the last afternoon with her. Her fevered two days of preparation would not be enough, for she hadn't had time to ask Frar to speak on behalf of the dead, or Astri to sing, or the fathers and brothers to teach the fledges all the constellations on Fourth Night . . . none of it would be done, because she was weak, because she had failed. Ketil and Maja would be happy to be right, and Ragna would be disappointed.

And Shard, her Vanir king . . .

"Shard." Cool fear washed her. She *had* overexerted, made herself sick, put their kit in jeopardy. Shard mumbled something about a few more moments, and tucked his head under his wing. Brynja sat, unmoving, ears ticking back and forth to the sounds of gryfons moving on different levels of the cliff. Her kit. Surely they would've woken her if something was wrong with the kit.

But maybe they didn't know.

Drawing a slow breath, she nudged Shard once more, nibbling at his neck feathers. "Shard, wake. The sun has set. The Long Night has begun and we must gather for the Mother's Night."

It was the very last thing Brynja wanted to do, and clearly, Shard as well. He lifted his head, and immediately stood, looking her over. Their nest was large, and well built, but standing together they almost filled it to overflowing. They would need to expand it as their kit grew. Through the dimness, she felt his eyes pierce her.

"How do you feel?"

Taking a moment to ponder it, Brynja nodded once. "Well enough. The kit . . ." She stopped, waiting, but didn't feel the kit move. "Well enough. I wore us both out."

"I wish you'd asked for help." His warm voice, like a summer wind through aspen leaves, both comforted and admonished her.

She dipped her head, but flattened her ears, submissive yet defiant. "Ragna said it was mine to do—"

"She meant it was yours to *lead,* not that you had to do every task yourself, running yourself to the ground without any sort of help."

"I had help," she fibbed. "Maja and Ketil made all the food preparations—"

Shard's tail lashed, flicking against her hind legs as if to make her sit back down. "I know you wanted to do everything yourself, but no one expected you to. And if you felt they did, then we all failed you. No one expected you to."

"But they did," Brynja insisted, ears still slanted back, as defensiveness and worry both clawed about in her breast. "They want to prove I'm not a proper queen for the Vanir by watching me fail—"

"Brynja," Shard said, lowering his head to meet her eyes solidly. "No one wants to see you fail. Sometimes I fear that *you're* the one who thinks you're not a proper queen for the Vanir."

It struck too close to the truth. A talon twisted her heart. Briefly, she missed her mother and her nest in the warm red rocks of the Dawn Spire. Outside, the wind moaned against the rocks, and it was as dark as the First Night of the world. She looked away from the shadow of Shard's face. "Maja and Ketil—"

"Gabbling magpies," Shard said, sounding exactly like his uncle, Stigr. She wondered what he would think of all this. She would have liked him there, and her aunt and mentor, Valdis. But they were over an impossible sea, and she had to do it alone.

Well, not truly alone. Shard went on. "They've actually done a lot to help, and you know that. As for you being my queen, Ketil would fuss and fret over any gryfess not of her personal choosing—whether Vanir, Aesir, half-blood, or some winged creature formed by Tor herself from moonlight and seawater."

Brynja choked out a laugh, and he butted his head fondly against her wing. A burst of longing for the days when she'd been light and spry enough to soar with him over the sea and the plains shot through her. She had to remind herself her pregnancy was very temporary, she had only a few more cold winter moons, then they would have their own warm rollicking kit to introduce to the world.

Her belly felt stiff, and still. She loosed a slow breath. "We should go. At the very least, I can't be late for the Mother's Night."

She let him believe he had soothed all her fears, that she didn't fear Maja or Ketil's disapproval. She didn't mention Ragna, who might as well have been Tor herself, for her distant, regal coolness. Shard was intelligent and compassionate and kind, but Brynja couldn't bring herself to set him against his own mother with her own suspicions, when they'd been forced into estrangement by the Conquering. Especially not now, during their most important celebration of the year.

Forcing her nerves to be calm, and her muscles to move against the stiffening, hard cold, she climbed the cliff trail with Shard behind her. It was exhausting to mind every step of the way, feeling for ice slicks in the dark.

Surprising, warm gold light flickered from the top of the cliffs, and she remembered that she'd wanted fires for the first night. For a moment she regretted the choice, which might seem disrespectful to the wishes of the Vanir. Then, as they topped the rise and came over the cliff, a freezing wind sucked the wind from her, and she felt better about having fire. She stopped short to catch a breath, then forced herself up and forward, making room for Shard.

Five bonfires raged against the dark and frosty air, in the sheltered protection of the King's Rocks, the jutting stones in the rough center of the nesting cliffs. They were perfectly laid out, and burning strong.

Brynja thought Dagny must have overseen the building of the fires, as she'd had such a role at the Dawn Spire back home.

Back at the Winderost, Brynja corrected herself. *This is my home.*

The wind made the fires swirl and dance, but the stone protected them just enough from guttering out. More than twenty gryfons clustered around each fire, over a hundred strong. The entire pride had left their nests for the first eve of the Long Night. Brynja felt a spark of hope.

Aesir and half-bloods gathered closest to the fires, talking amiably as if it were a summer night. Old Vanir hung back, ears twitching uncertainly, as if they couldn't decide whether to stay warm, or respect the ancient and freezing traditions of their ancestors. Their disapproval felt like an extra layer of cold wind to Brynja, and she ground her beak against a sigh.

"I like it," Shard said lightly, and her wings twitched in surprise. "And see how pleased the nestling mothers are."

Brynja looked again. It was true—mothers with fluffy nestlings curled up close to the flames, not having to worry that their little ones would freeze, and not having to miss the celebration by staying in their warm and sheltered nests. The fires made it possible for all to attend the Mother's Night—even the mothers.

Brynja felt slightly better. Even more so when she spied a glittering white gryfess with her nestling, close to the nearest fire. Astri, and little Eyvindr. Perhaps if the half-blood could accept the fire, she would accept the request to sing the next night . . . Fire caught on copper feathers nearby and Brynja tried to catch Dagr's gaze to see if he'd spoken to Astri yet, if he'd broken the ice. But he was letting Eyvindr wrestle against his talons, and didn't notice her. Beside Dagr sat his father, Vidar, one of the old Vanir, who looked determined to enjoy the fire for the sake of his remaining son. Brynja searched for Vidar's estranged mate, but saw Eyvin over by another fire, nearer to the other Aesir.

Before she could spot anyone else and gauge their reactions, Shard murmured in her ear. "Remember, you'll never make everyone happy. They're waiting for you to begin now."

Realization that the entire pride had fallen silent, and now stared at Brynja as she stared at them, made her chuckle self-consciously. "And I'm freezing. Let's go."

They strode together, side by side, into the light of the largest fire. Brynja found Dagny,

Sigrun, and Caj, and stood near them. She looked to Shard, but her young gray king held back, ears perked toward her.

Brynja hesitated, then turned from the fire and climbed, to much worried murmuring, up to the top of the King's Rocks, and turned to behold the pride. Her pride. From muttering Ketil to cautious Astri and handsome, curious Dagr, practical Sigrun and noble Caj . . . they were hers to protect and to lead. They might not have chosen her, but she had chosen them.

The wind buffeted her feathers, and she hoped she looked strong with the firelight from below, and the starlight on her back.

Cool, waiting looks from the Vanir met her gaze. Encouraging, yet doubtful sideways looks from the dragon-blessed, brightly colored Aesir. Hopeful, excited fledgling eyes gleamed back at her, and gave her the strength she needed. They had lived through a war, and now that there was peace, every new thing was an adventure, full of possibility.

"Welcome all to the first night of darkness," Brynja said, raising her voice over the wind and crackling flames. Wood smoke brought memories of her first nest, of her father and mother, of the red earth she'd flown from to make a home here. "I know the fire is a departure from the traditions of the Vanir, but I hope Tor knows we light them to honor her love of Tyr, the sun, the flame, and to allow those more frail among us to join the celebration." After a slight pause she added, "Including me, apparently."

She referenced her fainting spell and day-long sleep, and was rewarded with some knowing, hesitant laughter. She couldn't bring herself to find Ragna in the firelight, unsure what the old queen would think of her weakness and falling, and of the fire, and of everything.

She sucked a breath, bracing herself against the battering wind, and lifted her voice again. "This is the Mother's Night, and we gather to honor Tor as she rises, and with her, our huntress ancestors."

At last a small spark of approval seemed to warm amongst the Vanir onlookers. The fires were a departure from their traditions but this, at least, was familiar.

"I name En," Brynja said clearly into the smoke and wind. "Mother of the second oldest and proudest line of Aesir in the Winderost. Her love for a gryfon not of her own clan was the first of its kind, and helped us to shed false barriers between us. Because of En's courage and her honest heart, we have all grown stronger, and can love freely. In Tor's light, I honor her."

After a brief moment, letting herself be lit by fire, Brynja climbed down the King's Rocks and to Shard's side. His rumbling purr of approval eased her quivering muscles and racing heart.

He raised his voice next, but he didn't presume to climb the rocks on the Mother's Night. "I honor Freja, a gryfess I met in a dream. She sacrificed her life to save the life of a kit in her pride. A hard death, but a sacrifice any gryfon would be glad to make. I honor Freja, a queen of the Vanir."

After the Vanir nodded knowingly and the Aesir shifted uncomfortably at this mention of their king's uncanny visions, it fell quiet as they waited for another to speak. Brynja spied Ragna in the gathering, but the pale widow remained silent, her eyes unreadable.

"I honor Maj," Eyvin called at last from her far fires. "A noble gryfess of the Second Age who, along with En and others, established the noblest bloodlines of the Dawn Spire."

Encouraged now, other gryfons raised their voices, calling out their ancestors and deeds. Names flew past Brynja's ears. Some well known, some obscure, some recently passed—though not too recent, for that was for Third Night. Ancestors, queens, huntresses of great renown. Brynja longed to hear their full stories, and her heart pounded to think that one distant day, some gryfon might stand and name Brynja, daughter-of-Mar, red queen of the Silver Isles . . .

She shook her head. She had a lot to do if she wanted to be named on this night, and it was silly to think of doing deeds just for that. She had a pride to care for, a king, a kit . . . she listened to the history, to warrior males, pregnant females, huntresses and elders proudly naming their female ancestors.

At last when the fires lay low, and Brynja spied a crescent of stars rising on the horizon that Shard called the Talon, she knew it was close to midnight, and almost time for all to go to their rest.

But one gryfess still hadn't spoken. Gryfons looked around at each other, expectant, an air of anxiousness tightening the gathering. At last Brynja dared to find Ragna in the crowd, and watched her, unsure if she planned to name someone, or if the name she'd wanted to speak had been taken. Or maybe she disapproved of the fires and meant to show it by not participating. Brynja's heart quickened and she tightened her talons against the packed snow. Even Maja and Ketil had proudly named their own ancestors under the moon and stars.

Just when Brynja feared she might not speak after all, Ragna stood, and opened her pale wings against the fire light. Relief and worry clustered in Brynja's heart.

"I must name one who is not my own bloodline," Ragna said, her voice ringing strong in the night. The wind had long since died, and red embers glowed against the snow and still air. "She is not mine to claim, but we share a history, and there is no one here to name her." She lifted her gaze to the bright, glittering band that Shard called Midragur. "I honor the sacrifice of Elena, a queen of the Aesir. A huntress of the Aesir who followed her dragon-blessed mate, Sverin, and carried her own kit across the sea in the hopes of giving him a better life." Ragna's pale gaze traveled thoughtfully across the gathering. "She died in a noble but failed attempt to feed her family, in a desperate attempt to embrace the ways of the Vanir. She did it for pride, for love, and duty. She will never be forgotten." Ragna's green eyes drifted back across the utterly silent, stunned pride, and rested at last on Brynja. "I honor her," the queen said quietly, and though all heard, Brynja felt it could have been for her ears alone. "For the sacrifices she made to try to make a life here, the sacrifices she made for her family."

Brynja stood slowly on shaking legs. "May all your honors be carried on strong winds to Tor's ear. This ends our Mother's Night. Go to your rest. We observe the day when the Talon sets, and the Boar rises. Let us go to rest, and meet back again for the Second night when the stars of the Hawk are high."

The gryfons rose sleepily, seeming happy, tired, but warm and ready for their rest.

"Come my love," Shard murmured. "That was well done."

"Just a moment." Brynja nuzzled him. "I have two things to tend to."

She walked along a meandering but well-packed trail to the center fire to find Frar, who was still curled up, appearing to enjoy the warmth of the embers and the sight of the pride talking happily together.

"Ah, my lady," said the old gryfon. "I'm glad to see you well."

"Thank you for your help." She dipped her head. "I meant to find you earlier to ask you if . . ." it seemed suddenly difficult, and awkward, to ask a gryfon so close to his own flight to the Sunlit Land to speak for the dead, and she stopped, and stared at him blankly.

"Ragna mentioned you might ask me to speak on the Third Night," Frar said quietly, his voice like dry leaves in the wind.

Brynja lifted a foot in surprise, taken aback. *Ragna asked him for me?* She hoped this wasn't a break in tradition, and that the queen knew Brynja had meant to ask before she'd fainted. She realized Frar watched her expectantly, and that she hadn't, in fact, officially asked him. Heat flamed under the feathers of her face.

"Honored Frar, will you speak for the gryfons who passed on to the Sunlit Land this year, not in battle, but on other winds?"

The old gryfon dipped his scruffy head, his fathers fluffing up in pleasure. "I would be very honored. I will need someone to give me the names of the Aesir who have passed, for my memory isn't what it might be."

"I will—"

"*I* will," insisted a gryfess from behind Brynja. She turned to see Eyvin, Dagr's mother, striding forward through the snow. Behind her stood Vidar, and Brynja felt hopeful that they'd been speaking to each other. Eyvin mantled when she drew closer. "With all due respect my lady, I hope you will rest, and let the rest of us help you now."

Brynja looked from her to Frar, then back, and noted the sparks of amusement and concern in both their fierce eyes. Finally, also feeling Shard's eyes on her from paces away, she lowered her head. "Thank you. I accept."

"Go to your nest," Eyvin said briskly. "Frar and I will speak."

After only a moment's hesitation, Brynja left them, though not for her nest. She trotted after a disappearing pale form. Astri walked from the fire, with Eyvindr riding tucked between her wings. Brynja expected to see the young gryfon sleeping, but he sat awake, staring around with wide eyes.

"Astri," Brynja said

The white gryfess stopped, turning to offer a careful mantle without dislodging Eyvindr. "My lady."

"M'ady," Eyvindr echoed from her shoulders.

"Eyvindr," Brynja said, her heart flaring with warmth. The kit ruffled his feathers proudly, then whipped his head to watch a spark that floated past him and up into the sky. Brynja paused, Astri watching her expectantly, and loosed her request in a single quick breath. "Astri, I was hoping to ask you about leading the singing on the Second Night."

"Dagr mentioned the singing." Her gaze drifted from Brynja to the copper gryfon who, Brynja understood, looked very much like Einarr had. He laid side by side with Tollak, and Caj near them, all reminiscing further on great gryfons and gryfesses they had known.

"Say you will," Brynja said softly, drawing Astri's attention back to her. A pang lanced her heart at the sight of distant sadness in her eyes. How Astri must miss her mate at a time like this—dark winter, and their first big celebration after years of fear and terror of this time of year. "Please," Brynja added. "It would mean a great deal to everyone, especially to me."

Quiet eyes met hers, and Brynja realized how young Astri was—how young Einarr must have been. Sparks popped from the nearby embers, and Brynja shivered against the cold of midnight.

"I will," Astri whispered tightly. "Because Einarr loved Shard, and Shard loves you. My lady."

"M'ady," Eyvindr said, stretching his growing wings.

"Thank you," Brynja said, as warmly as she could.

Without further comment, Astri dipped her head and walked on toward the cliff trail and her nest.

To stay her own sadness, Brynja found Shard, and together they bid good night to gryfons they passed as they went to their rest.

As they curled up, Shard spoke quietly. "If you'll let me, tomorrow I'll speak to others to help arrange the rest of the nights. I'm sure Mother would help you too. She's done this before you know, but she doesn't want to intrude."

"She doesn't?" Brynja fluffed up the hide at the bottom of the nest—a gift from

Ahanu, the wolf king. "I thought she was disappointed in me, or waiting to see if I did everything right."

Shard laughed, then stopped quickly when he realized she was serious. "How could you think she would leave you to do everything alone? She thought you *wanted* to do it all yourself. If anyone tried to help you, you fluffed up like a jaybird on its nest and looked ready to attack."

"I suppose I did want to do it myself." Brynja eased down to her side, careful of her belly. "But I know I can't, now. Tell her I would welcome her counsel?"

Shard tucked in next to her and laid his head on her wing. "I think you should tell her yourself. It would mean a lot to her."

Brynja felt a purr rising in her chest. Perhaps all the time she thought Ragna was being distant, the widow was trying to give Brynja space to be her own queen . . . "I will," she mumbled, and fell to sleep, dreaming fretfully of the next "day's" preparations, and a kit with wings made of fire . . .

Morning came, but it was night. It was dark. Brynja and the pride moved strangely, as if in a dream, and she stared at stars she'd never seen before.

After speaking with Ragna about the rest of the celebration, she was able to take a little more time to rest, confident that others could help her see to the details. Watching Maja and Ketil help the Widow Queen, she slowly realized that they didn't want to control what Brynja did, but only to be noticed, involved, and remembered.

In the dark, she became intimate with the stars, watching them as she would've watched the sun pass overhead.

The Second Night festivities filled the Sun Isle with song. Astri's pure, sweet voice led them off with a traditional Vanir lullaby that

Brynja hadn't yet heard. They called it "The Starward Light."

> *The shortest day is done*
> *The Long Night has begun*
> *But fear not, my love, the dark*
> *The dark*
> *The darkness can be bright.*
> *Behold the starward light*
> *Behold the longest, brightest night.*
>
> *We rest as winter winds blow*
> *We sing as the darkness grows*
> *Fear not my love the cold*
> *The cold*
> *We will make the cold warm and bright*
> *Behold the starward light . . .*

Brynja found herself humming the melody throughout the following day, and into the Third Night, when they honored the dead. It was a quiet affair. Brynja learned that the gathered rowan berries were collected in honor of the dead, and the Vanir used to cast them into the sea. This night, Vanir did so for their dead, but the Aesir cast theirs into the fires, and another new tradition was born. Clouds blotted their stars, and snow flurried around the gathering.

Brynja watched Caj's face as he named those who'd died in battle that year, including Einarr, including Sverin. For each name he added a virtue, and cast a red berry into the fire.

Frar remained seated to name the dead who'd passed by natural causes, but their number was few. The fire popped and sizzled as snow struck it. Through unspoken agreement they lit fires each night to hold the dark at bay.

Some mutterings and disapproval came to Brynja, from the Vanir. How were they to honor the night and dark if they kept lighting fires? But they'd been in cold darkness for so long, and nightmares followed some of the gryfons when all the light went out. Sigrun had confessed to Brynja that Caj struggled against memories of Sverin and the king's suffering during the Long Night, and how the light of the fires eased his anxiousness. Brynja never would have guessed by the old warrior's bearing and stoic face that he suffered any unease.

But many of the old Vanir grew unhappier as the twelve days went on.

The Fourth Night, when they taught the fledges the stars and the stories, the Vanir had to lead them farther from the nesting cliffs and the fires so all the stars could be seen. Brynja remained close to the flames, though Shard went with the others.

She felt Maja, Ketil, and others' eyes on her, as if waiting for her to extinguish the fires. She refused. The warmth was doing good for herself and the other expectant mothers, and those who were afraid of the dark.

Besides, if Ragna or Shard had any doubts about her choice, they didn't speak it, so she assumed they agreed.

Or perhaps they were just letting her lead in her own way.

You'll never make everyone happy, Shard had said. The more Brynja told herself that, the more the voice sounded like Valdis, then herself, less practical and more critical.

You'll never make anyone happy . . .

They ran through their wood stores quickly and sent out gryfons, in the dark, to gather more wood for the rest of the nights. Dagr and the others seemed happy to oblige, though Brynja learned of Vidar and other's disapproval from Shard after the celebrations of the Fifth night.

"It's too cold," she argued, though she also feared what the Aesir might do if they were faced with the dark without the fire to shield them. She couldn't ignore the memory of the wyrms, of the nightmarish period of silence and fasting and darkness Shard told her the pride had endured for the last ten years. "I thought they'd be happy to have the fire."

"They are," Shard said quietly, tucking hides about her and fidgeting with the pine boughs. "But . . . balance in all things. How can the Aesir learn not to fear the night if they never really experience it?"

"The Long Night is mine to lead. And I choose to have light in the dark." She huffed and settled, staring out of their den where the faint glow of firelight could still be seen from above.

For a moment Shard was quiet, then he said, "Do you remember when we flew above the fires of the Dawn Spire so that I could show you the stars?"

Warmth swept down Brynja's back. How she remembered. "So you could ask me to mate with you, you mean?"

Shard chuckled, but perked his ears, refusing to be blown off course. "It was then you also saw there was light in the dark."

Brynja lowered her head, tail twitching once. He was right. But she knew how the Aesir had suffered in the dark . . .

"I honor your choice," Shard said quietly, sitting. "As does the rest of the pride."

Brynja nodded once, though she felt uneasy. Her kit had moved a little, but seemed sluggish compared to the fall, and she worried she'd harmed it from her over-exertion. "Will you sing to me?"

Shard laughed quietly. In honor of the season he began, *"The shortest day is done, the Long Night has begun . . ."*

They woke the next black, starry "morning" to commotion on top of the cliffs. Gryfon voices raised—some in protest, some in happiness and surprise. Shard jostled Brynja with apologies as he scrambled out of the nest toward the sound of growing arguments.

Brynja stretched carefully and trundled up the cliff trail to find him, and all the fuss. Their pride mates had returned not just with fire wood, but meat. Red meat, and birds.

"This is blasphemous and disrespectful!" Ketil's voice cracked through the dark. "Already we can barely see the stars because of the fires. Now you would feed us with the same food forced on the pride by the conquerors?" Apparently catching scent of Brynja, Ketil whirled, eyes fierce. "We have not once seen the Wings of Tor this winter, surely it's a sign—"

"A sign of nothing," growled old Frar from somewhere in the dark. "I saw several years without the Wings of Tor in my day. Ketil, remember you speak to your queen."

Dagny oozed around Brynja, brushing a reassuring wing against her as she went to stoke the fires.

"I wish only for my queen to respect our ways. We will *not* eat red—"

"It was a gift," Dagr said evenly, still holding a ptarmigan. "A gift, from the king and queen of the Star Isle. They've seen our fires and heard our songs over the water, and wished us a happy Long Night. It's as simple as that."

Ketil fell silent, and fuming. Brynja eyed the meat with longing, but in this, she looked to Shard.

The gray king dipped his head a little, and she saw him searching the faces of the gathered gryfons, seeking out the desires of the pride. There was a clear line of response between the Aesir and the Vanir. After a moment, she realized he was watching her now.

Because it was still the Long Night, he meant for her to decide.

Brynja's belly snarled. She was certain that hearty red meat would do her sluggish kit some good, but she also felt the icy and expectant stares from Ketil and other Vanir. She thought of what Ketil said, about not having seen the Wings of Tor—the brilliant aurora that usually lit the night skies. Her dream haunted her again, of a sun that wouldn't set, and she wondered if there could ever really be balance in their pride.

Balance in all things.

She opened her wings, feeling cold wind brush under her feathers. She had her fires. The Vanir needed something too. "We'll send word to the wolves that we accept their generous gift—"

Grumbles and shouts rose, and Brynja narrowed her eyes, loosing a snarl to silence them.

"We will accept their generous gift, freeze it in the ice near the shore, and partake of it *after* the Long Night is done. I know how important the vows of the Vanir are."

Low murmurs. She saw ears twitching against the starlight. But no one could find a protest to raise against that. To return a well-meant gift—or worse, waste food, would be a more awful crime than eating it a bit later, surely they could see that.

Shard approach Brynja and nuzzled behind her ears. "Well done," he murmured. "I know you want the meat. Thank you for waiting."

"For you and them," she said quietly. "I can wait. Now, walk with me please. I have an idea for the Twelfth Night, but I'll need your help."

After that, the energy of the pride waned with the moon, which had been half full at the beginning of the Long Night. The wind shuddered the darkness around them, rattled the dry and stripped branches of the birch, and froze the shallow banks of the Nightrun.

The sea shushed and moaned with forming and cracking ice.

Clouds obscured their stars for multiple days of murky dark, glowing violet with their fires when they deemed it was evening time.

Brynja strained not to wallow in the dark, and was grateful for the second half of the nightly celebrations. The Sixth night they sang lullabies, mother's songs, which reminded her that the earth needed time to rest and restore, and that the sun would come again.

It seemed it would never end—but it was only a long night, not an endless night.

She had to remember that.

At last, when only a sliver of moon rose and set, it was the Twelfth Night. A strained and sun-starved pride met Brynja's welcome under the starlight and the fire. Shard and others were ready to help her enact a plan she hoped would make the Vanir happy on the last night of their celebration. Ketil had managed to stir unease, talking about the firelight insulting Tor, driving off the very goddess they hoped to honor.

Brynja would hope the great mother would understand their need for warmth in the dark. She hoped her last act during the Long Night would appease some of the unhappiness.

"It is the last evening of darkness," Brynja called from the top of the King's Rocks. "Welcome, my pride. My family. Tomorrow we will see a true sunrise again."

Some grumbled. Many were ready to be well shed of the exuberant, but exhausting celebrations in the unending dark, yet there was a strange regret too. The darkness gave excuse for longer periods of rest and time in their nests with their families. The kits and fledglings remained unruffled and excited, playing games of hide and seek in the snow and firelight.

"We thank the stars for helping us to track the days," Brynja said, her voice firm and hard against the frosty cold and black air. Ears remained tuned to her. "We thank Tor for her light and her guidance. We thank the sea for unending bounty. I thank our hunters, our warriors, our fathers and mothers for their strength and the light in their hearts. And thank all of you for allowing me to lead this Long Night, for accepting my need for warmth and fire in the darkness, though it goes against the oldest traditions. I hope we will find balance in all things."

She took a deep breath, listened to the quiet mutters and exclamations. "We are a new pride, making new traditions, so let this be one. On this night, we know the sun will rise again tomorrow. This night, we sit vigil to wait for the sun, because we know Tyr will rise again." Cold wind raked at her ears and she sucked a breath against it. "The days will grow longer and spring will come. So, let us observe the final eve of the Long Night as we were meant to. We will honor the Twelfth Night vigil for the dawn as the Vanir have for long centuries . . . in the dark."

She had planned ahead with Shard, Dagny, and others, and warned those who might be sensitive to the cold as to her plan, but all had chosen to leave their warm nests and attend.

When she flared her wings, gryfons moved forward to douse the flames with snow, plunging the pride into utter blackness. Gasps and a few happy calls, and unhappy, met her ears, a few moments of wing-ruffling chaos.

Then, they went still. Brynja waited, with them. Gradually their eyes widened and adjusted to the fireless dark.

One by one, faces turned skyward. Vanir, Aesir. The littlest kits.

Brynja looked up, felt warmth at her side as Shard joined her, and with a shiver of awe, saw that indeed it was the brightest night.

The stars, unhindered by the light of the fires, blazed forth with the might and shocking intensity of the First Light that had ever touched the world. Midragur, the dragon stars, slashed across the sky, revealed in layers of white starlight, violet sky, and streaks of distant copper fire. The Swan flew high above all, a guide. The immense blackness and unending shower of stars seemed, for a moment, as if they would consume Brynja and all the pride. She grounded herself by finding stars she knew—the wolf stars, the High Pack. The Mare. The Talon hovered near the horizon, and Brynja knew the Long Night was almost done.

No one spoke.

A gentle, frigid wind caressed them, but she felt the warmth of the pride.

A pale presence approached, and without having to look and catch a scent, Brynja turned and mantled to Ragna. "Thank you for supporting me," she whispered, unable to raise her voice against the overwhelming night.

"Thank *you*," the white gryfess said quietly, and it was all Brynja needed to hear. She stood tall again, and they turned their faces to the sky.

A new light flickered, a faint spear of color. It died . . . then wisped again, like a ripple across the night.

Brynja sucked in a sharp breath, and held it.

A bolt of green shot over the White Mountains and unfurled like a shining emerald wing across the sky. Luminous rose glowed and undulated in silken sheets along the green, and the stars dimmed behind the display.

"The Wings of Tor," Shard breathed, and his voice made her shiver. "I've never seen them so bright."

Brynja stared, enveloped in impossible light, color, and dazzling movement as if the goddess flapped slow, divine wings over their heads.

Cries of joy resounded in the night. Gryfons leaped forward and up into the air to fly and dance in the light.

A pale form swooped past with a call of "Well done!" as if Brynja herself had summoned the light. She realized after a stunned moment that it was Ragna, praising her again, and more unrestrained in her joy than Brynja had never seen her before.

The Widow Queen led a flight high into the very light of the Wings, and Brynja's heart flamed and grew and flew with them.

In her belly, the kit shifted in a quick surge, kicking and flaring with renewed strength, as if the light shining on Brynja's face had poured through her into its heart. She was certain, certain then, that her kit would be a huntress, a queen.

Silhouettes of flying, exulting gryfons darted about in the caress of the shifting lights, and joy radiated from the entire pride like the warmth from a massive fire. The Vanir swooped over her head and thanked her, even

Maja, even Ketil. Half-bloods joined them, and even a scattering of Aesir, including Caj and Eyvin. The coppery gryfess met Vidar in the sky, and they swooped around each other in hesitant circles, like younger gryfons on the Daynight. Brynja felt hopeful they might reunite as mates, or perhaps even just mend their wounds as friends.

The very young and old remained near the fires. Brynja saw Pala curled up next to Frar, and he, surrounded by adoring nestlings and fledges who loved his stories. Astri remained on the ground with Eyvindr, watching the Wings with shining eyes.

Brynja leaned into Shard, letting herself relax at last under the Wings of Tor, and waited for the dawn.

"He passed in the first light," Pala murmured to Brynja and Shard. They stood together in the healer's den, over the still and peaceful body of Frar. The apprentice had summoned her to inform her of his death in the night. Sigrun and Idunn had flown to the Star Isle to gather what herbs could be found in the new light of day, and they were alone in the den.

He waited for the Long Night, Brynja thought with a surge of sadness, but also strange relief. He earned his rest. She lifted a wing to cover Shard's back, for she knew what the old gryfon had meant to him. Frar was the first exiled Vanir Shard had found in the Winderost, the first to come to his beacon, and the most stalwart in making the long and difficult flight home.

"He told me how pleased he was with your celebration," the young healer murmured to Brynja, then addressed both of them, formally. "He wanted to celebrate one last Long Night in his home. He died without pain, in his sleep, and Tyr's first light summoned him to the Sunlit Land."

Brynja looked at the apprentice healer, at her startling but appropriate colors, like blood and starlight, and thought what good healers she and Idunn would make for the pride in their futures together.

"Thank you for caring for him," Shard said, dipping his head to Pala. His voice grated, tight, as if he'd swallowed gravel. Brynja pressed close to his side. "I'm glad he had good company on his last night."

"He will be the first we name next winter," Brynja said quietly, gently running her talons over the old gryfon's head, as if he were a kit. "When we honor the dead on the Third Night."

"Very good, my lady," Pala said, then looked to Shard. Her gaze was quiet, serene, a healer's inscrutable expression. She and Idunn had grown up fast after the wyrms attacked, Brynja thought grimly. "Shall I summon warriors to bear him to Black Rock?"

Shard gazed at Frar. "No, I'll find them, and help bear him myself."

"Yes, my lord," Pala said, and mantled low.

"Go," Brynja said to Shard, when he looked at her with concern. "I'll be fine." She looked beyond him to the growing light outside the den. She thought of the long days of darkness, of the passing seasons, of losing one gryfon after a long life, and of the new lives that would come in spring. They could turn outward again now, do what work needed to be done, be grateful for each other, and for the light.

And the dark.

"Go," she said again to Shard, lifting her voice. "He wouldn't want you to be sad, on such a beautiful morning."

"'Yes, my lady." Shard loosed a weak chuckle, nuzzled her ear, and left the den.

Brynja touched her beak to Frar's head, then brushed a comforting wing tip against Pala's shoulder, and they walked together into the fresh silver light of a new winter's day.

-oOo-

Beneath the Windward Sun

A Tale of the Winderost

Jess E. Owen

The Voldsom Narrows echoed with the murmurings of hundreds of gryfons. The eagles had woken early, and already hunted along the hazy canyon rim farther starward. Stigr stood with Shard, striving to remember everything he'd wanted to tell his nephew before he flew away.

His last recommendation that Shard try to stay alive met with some resistance.

"I would die for any of them," Shard said, eyes narrowing.

Stigr kept his tone even, admiring the audacity of youth. "I know, Shard. So do they.

But they don't need you to die, they need you to *live*. A living king is better than a dead one. Remember that."

"Stigr—"

"A living king," he said again, very quietly, and watched his nephew take a slow, measured breath. His green eyes, Ragna's eyes, grew distant as they did when Shard was remembering something, or experiencing a vision.

"My father," he said, as if coming to a new realization. "You don't think he should have challenged Per."

The hardened grief tore open, just a little, like the raw scar where his wing had once been. He hadn't been thinking of Baldr directly, but once Shard said it, Stigr knew he was right—and he remembered. And he told him, because Shard deserved to know. "I told him not to, but I think he believed it was best at the time." Fresh sadness pooling about his heart, Stigr forced himself to add, "But that's long done."

"It is," Shard said, looking encouraged by Stigr's apparent willingness to let go the past, making Stigr glad he'd said it, glad to make Shard believe all was well with him.

Then, neither spoke again.

Wind drifted, stirring the scent of dust, frost, and all their allies.

Shard, looking ragged and weary and every inch a king-to-be, stood as still as an uncertain fledgling, awaiting direction.

Stigr shifted, trying to think of some other sliver of advice, some word, something to draw out this last parting. He didn't know when they would see each other again, or even if. He waited for Shard to say something, to draw himself together, to turn at last to the mass of gryfons patiently waiting for his word.

But after another moment of heavy silence, Stigr knew his nephew needed him, one last time.

"It's time, Shard." He backed away a step, then another, forcing earth and wind between them. "It's time."

Taking a long breath, Shard turned, extending his wing toward Stigr's good side. Fresh surprise swooping through his chest, Stigr opened his wing to eclipse it as Shard spoke.

"Fair winds, Uncle."

"Fair winds, my prince." It felt strange to say it now, and somehow, that word wasn't enough. Wasn't right. Regret forced itself out in a laugh and Stigr added, "My friend."

Shard met his gaze one last time, turned, and hoarsely shouted the order to fly.

The sight of the exiled Vanir taking wing first pierced Stigr's heart with triumph, then darker remorse. He would never join them. His task was done, his life's purpose for last ten years flew now beyond his reach, and he watched his pride fly home without him. It took every fiber of strength in his muscles not to race after them on the ground, to follow until his legs or his heart gave out.

Then . . .

Just when he needed her, Valdis came, pressing to his lame side, adding the warmth and weight he missed with his wing.

"You did well by him," she said, her own voice chalky and flat. "Your part is done. Don't say the valiant warrior I chose will become a sulking crow now that your nephew has achieved all you hoped he would."

Stigr, pulling himself out of the mire, realized she had just bid farewell to Brynja, her own niece and the closest she would ever have to a daughter. Neither of them could very well wallow. Kits grew, and fledged, and the flew the nest. Even if Shard's nest was farther away than Stigr would have liked, it was the way of the world.

He buried his beak in the feathers behind Valdis' ear. "Come." He looked dawnward. "Let's go . . . home."

Stigr clutched a rock outcropping, hauling himself up the narrow, winding way to the top of the Wind Spire. Already, moist heat pounded the dark morning, and a long blanket of gray cloud swept from the Dawn Spire to all the far horizons. A sliver of orange under the far end of the cloud bank promised a stifling day.

The lancing cramp in his wingless shoulder told Stigr it might very rain, later, and that would be a welcome relief, even if the changes in wind and pressure brought him aches. The late days of summer wore on him, and he longed for the chilly days of winter. Biting back grumbles, he worked himself carefully up the trail. It was actually not quite a *trail*, but a climbing trek he had devised to prove to Kjorn, Asvander, and the rest of the Guard that he could stand a watch like anyone else.

The trickiest part came near the top, where the rock proved too hard to carve a trail, and he had a near-vertical ascent for the length of two lion's leaps. Though he'd been doing it for years now, it proved a challenge every day.

Gathering his resolve and trying to ignore the sharp pain in his shoulder that was worming its way up his neck, Stigr gathered his hind legs and jumped to the first talon-hold. It was best to move quickly and not think too much, using the power of confidence and motion. Grasping rock and catching his hind claws on feather-fine ridges in the stone, he scrambled up the tower like a squirrel up a juniper.

He grasped the ridge that widened into the lookout post, and was about to haul himself over the top when a stabbing pain in his shoulder made him cry out, and his talons seized, flexing and releasing. He swung down, hanging by three talons and his hind claws.

His wing flared.

Now, even now, his wing betrayed him, flaring instinctively to fly. Instead, it threw him off balance, rolling him sideways along the vertical face of rock, twisting his other foreleg as he strained to keep hold of the ledge.

His back slammed against the stone and he lost his grip. The sickening lurch of falling into open air halted with a wrenching jerk in his wrist joint.

Strong talons had snatched his foreleg, then the other, then released his foot and grabbed him by the shoulder, digging into the numb scar. Stigr managed to shut his wing against a gust of wind. With the help of the sentry on the rock and strong, scrabbling shoves with his hind legs, together they pulled up him and over to splay across the wide, flat surface of the lookout post.

"That was invigorating. A way to keep me alert, for certain."

"Fair winds, Rok," Stigr muttered, rolling to his feet.

"Fair winds, my friend." The tall, lanky brown gryfon sat, watching Stigr collect himself. "All's quiet, though I thought I spied lions earlier, but hard to tell without the light. Keep an eye windward."

Stigr noticed he didn't mention him almost falling again, but watched him suspiciously. Rok was one of three gryfons at the Dawn Spire who knew better than to suggest Stigr might consider taking his watch on a shorter tower. Stigr wanted the Wind Spire. He could climb it, he did climb it, he *had* climbed it, every morning for the last three years, and he wouldn't stop now because of a cramp.

"You're pretending to know what I'm thinking again," Rok said. Stigr realized he'd been staring fiercely at the other gryfon, daring him to speak.

"No," Stigr said, relaxing his glare, perking his ears and peering around. The Wind Spire was the highest point of the aerie, aside from the Dawn Spire of course. Standing atop it in the wind, with the Winderost spread out below him, almost gave him the feeling of flying again, and a pleasant flutter in his heart. "I *know* what you're thinking, you and everyone else."

Rok stood and stretched, and Stigr wished he'd take his leave. But he didn't, and Stigr didn't ask him to. Aside from Asvander and Valdis, Rok was one of the few gryfons at the Dawn Spire Stigr had grown close to, would call a friend—a good friend, even. They respected each other. The former rogue had followed Kjorn to the Silver Isles and back, fought in the Battle of Pebble's Throw *and* the Battle of Torches before, as well as serving as ambassador to the free gryfons of the Winderost. Stigr had accompanied him to the First Plains and the Dawn Reach before, to speak to lions, rogue gryfons, and painted wolves, and never once had Rok complained that Stigr's presence meant the journey took three times as long.

There was more to him than his breezy attitude, so Stigr gave him more consideration than he might any other blunt, cocky gryfon.

Rok tilted his head. "You know what I'm thinking, eh? All right then prophet, have a go."

"You're thinking I'm still trying to prove a point by standing the watch, and you think it'd be safer if I didn't."

Rok laughed, a rich, booming laugh that probably woke half the gryfons not already stirring. "That's not what I'm thinking, that's just *true*. Care to know what I really think?"

"I think I'm about to hear whether I want to or not." Stigr flicked an ear his way though, curious despite himself.

"What I think is, you're wasting valuable energy and time when you could be serving the king and the Spire in a better way. How much earlier do you have to rise before dawn to make it up here in time for your post? What happens the next time you slip, and I'm not there to catch you? What would your nephew think when he returns someday, only to hear—"

"It's my choice." Irritation needled him, and his pride flared, but he knew Rok was right. Like him, Rok had once been an unwilling exile, a rogue living in the wilderness without his pride, though he seemed to have taken to it better than Stigr ever did. It gave them something to talk about anyway. Rok always seemed to find him around the fire in the evening and they talked into the night—which meant he was coming to know Stigr all too well.

"It won't be your choice for long," Rok said, more quietly. "If the king hears you almost fell."

Stigr eyed him. "Will the king hear?"

Rok fluffed his wing feathers in a shrug. "Not from me."

Stigr wasn't entirely sure he trusted that, but he had no alternative. "I hear you're leading a good-will visit to the Vanheim Shore before winter."

Rok's hackle feathers puffed up at the ungraceful change of subject, then he shook himself, sleeked, and chuckled, averting his gaze. "We want to keep good relations."

"I'm sure you do." Stigr thought of Shard, and of Sigrun, and of choices he'd never made that were made for him, in the end. "Rok, my friend. She's waiting, but she won't wait forever."

Rok's ears ticked back, and his tail flicked once. "We both know it wouldn't work. I can't leave the Dawn Spire now, and Nilsine would never leave the Vanheim."

"Do you know that?" Stigr stood, an old anger that had nothing to do with Rok roiling up under his skin, his scars, pounding in the place where he'd once possessed an eye. "Have you ever asked her? Have you ever made your heart known, even given her a choice?"

"She knows," Rok mumbled, and Stigr remembered how much younger he was.

"She does not. Tell her. Give her the choice. Then it will be decided one way or another, but you will have at least made a decision and it won't just fade, or end, or be taken from you."

"I suppose you would know." Rok glanced at him sideways, and the wind ruffled their feathers, smelling heavily of damp earth and ozone. Stigr knew he hadn't meant the words to cut, yet they did. The rogue was aware of his history—never mating with the gryfess he'd loved in the Silver Isles, and losing her to a conquering Aesir. Of course, that had resulted in other, happier things, but it was a long time in coming.

"As for choices . . ." Rok 's voice was firm, but the words cautious as he changed the subject again. "Have you thought any more on my—"

"I have," Stigr said quietly. "It's not a good time."

One ear flattened in disappointment, then Rok lashed his tail. "That's no answer. And here you speak of giving everyone straight answers and choices. There will never be a good time, Stigr. The answer is yes or no."

Stigr lifted his wing a little, for he didn't have a yes or no answer yet to the question Rok had asked a year ago, then again in the spring, and the summer again.

It just wouldn't do.

But that wasn't what Rok wanted to hear, so Stigr hadn't told him. "Thank you for the help. Go to your rest. I have the watch."

Rok's ears laid back, then he ducked his head once and jumped from the spire, gliding down in the muggy air toward his nest. Stigr wallowed in a moment of longing for his own wings, then turned to look over the land, alert for Rok's supposed lions or other trespassers, and hoping the rain held off until he'd finished his watch and climbed down.

Of course, it didn't.

ALVISS, THE ELDER HEALER, clicked his beak in a steady rhythm of disapproval as he secured an herb poultice in place on Stigr's hind hip. A trio of somber fledges watched every flick of his talons, except one, who stared at Stigr with her beak open. Stigr winced as the old gryfon tightened the sinew, then released a breath as the potent desert thornapple seeped into his bruised muscles.

"Three leaps you fell!" Valdis paced in the entryway, and rain beat a steady drum on the red stone of the aerie outside.

"Hardly that."

"Asvander saw you." Valdis turned, ears flat and eyes flashing. "He's not one for exaggeration. He said it was three leaps and you tumbled the whole way down. What were you thinking? You could have died. You could have broken something."

Stigr grumbled.

What's left to break?

Kits hollered and shrieked from the swollen stream that wound past the healer's den, splashing and searching for fish that weren't there. Stigr hoped someone was watching them, in case of flash flood. He eyed Valdis, knowing her hen-fussing only came from worry, but still, he wondered that she couldn't wait until they were out of the healer's den to humiliate him. Still he loved her, this gryfess who had vowed to be his mate even without him being able to fly in a proper ceremony, who had pledged her love to him on the ground.

Like lions, she had reassured him on that Daynight two years past. *Like the wolves you respect so.*

He could scarcely grudge her worry, this gryfess who understood him so well, who stood by him.

"I wouldn't have died," he said at length, quietly.

Alviss grumbled indelicately, as if clearing something from his throat. "You know, Stigr, the elders have been talking. Did you know Master Lenvir is thinking of joining—"

"Back in the evening for a fresh poultice?" Stigr rolled to his feet. He did not want a single suggestion that it was time for him to retire from sentry duty, nor especially that he should join the elders' circle. The elders indeed. As if he were even old enough, and good for nothing else but dispensing his hard-earned wisdom. He had many good fighting years left, and more wisdom yet to earn.

Alviss' tail flicked. He cast Valdis a sideways look and she ruffled her wing feathers indifferently. "Yes," said the healer. "Come back this evening before you eat, and again before your post in the morning. I'll make sure one of these lot has your poultice ready. I don't suppose I can convince you to take a day of rest and avoid climbing for a couple of . . . no, I thought not."

"Thank you," Stigr said, and left the den with Valdis. The rain lessened to a soft drizzle, and Stigr tried not to think if he'd waited but another quarter mark atop the Wind Spire, he might have had an easier climb down. He glanced at Valdis, and wondered if she was thinking the same. Her stony silence suggested he not strike up conversation. They walked along the canyon floor, and Stigr felt the strength and comfort of the walls that towered above their heads.

"Son of Ragr!" piped a small voice from behind.

Stigr paused and turned to see one of the apprentice healers bounding after them. "Yes, does Alviss need something?"

"No," said the young gryfess. She looked barely four. She would've been a nestling when he first came to the Dawn Spire. "Did you really fall three leaps from the ground?"

Eyeing Valdis, Stigr answered, "Yes."

"Tyr made you so strong," she breathed, eyes widening impossibly further. "I helped with your poultice. I hope it makes you feel better. I—I wanted to give you this." She thrust a delicate white flower in his face.

Stigr took a step back, then sniffed it. It didn't smell herby, or useful in a way that he knew of. "Ah, what is it for?"

She blinked large golden eyes and her neck hackle fluffed up self-consciously. "Oh. Just, for um . . . luck?" Apparently overcome by the question, she dropped the flower and fled back to the healer's den.

"Desert poppy," said Valdis, and picked the stem up carefully in her talons. "I don't know about luck, but many young gryfesses like to decorate their nests with it. I believe she's taken with you."

Stigr laughed, and submitted to allowing Valdis to tuck the flower behind his ear. "I could be her father. Twice."

Valdis snorted. "A harmless turning of the head. Though I can't imagine what she sees in you." A nibble at his neck feathers and Stigr knew Valdis had passed from anger at his foolish choices to relief that he hadn't broken his neck.

He should be flattered by a young gryfon's awe, yet somehow, the whole thing nettled him. He was nothing to aspire to or admire. Lame on an entire side of his body from both missing wing and eye, the only full-blooded Vanir in a pride of a thousand Aesir and half-bloods, growing older, and apparently less able . . . it wasn't long until Kjorn and his queen changed from actually needing him to humoring him, or worse, taking pity . . .

"Stop scowling," Valdis purred. "It makes you look old. Come, why don't we watch the lighting of the fires, and—"

"I'm going hunting," Stigr said, and didn't bother to look at her to see the expression he knew was there. Anger at being interrupted, disapproval at the idea of him leaving the aerie while injured.

Her wing came over his back. "Stigr—"

"I just need to walk this out."

"Then I'll come with you." Her wing tightened against his flank.

Stigr shifted. "I need some air. I'll be back."

"When?"

"Two days at most."

"Your poultice—"

"It's not as bad as he makes it out to be, my mate." He touched his beak quickly to her ear and slid out from under her wing, picking a trail at random he knew would lead him out of the aerie. She knew him well enough, loved him well enough, that she didn't protest, didn't call after him, and didn't follow.

BY SUNSET, THE RAIN had cleared to a smattering of dreary clouds and listless, dim evening sky. What sun there was cast long shadows over the red and ochre landscape, damp and dark. Stigr hobbled along after a fresh rabbit trail, stubbornly ignoring the increased throbbing in his hind leg. A fresh poultice would've helped, but he was closer to the rabbit den than the aerie by now, and he'd told Valdis two days. He couldn't very well go back after a single afternoon and admit both defeat at hunting and surrender to pain.

Pain is a sign of life, Baldr's father had told him once. Stigr tried to remember if he'd ever told that to Shard.

"The lack of pain," Stigr grunted, "means Tyr has taken you under his wing, and you might as well . . ."

A cool breeze picked up and he froze as the warm, red-meat scent of rabbit drifted across his nostrils. He'd developed a taste for red meat, though, like the wolves, he still observed the proper respect when he killed. He had to.

At the thought of Catori, of the Star Isle, of the sweet pines and the scent of the ocean, such unexpected longing and regret washed over Stigr that he forgot the rabbit briefly and sank to the ground.

When he stopped, every aching muscle and bruise from his fall caught up to him, and his legs threatened to cramp from his loping run into the desert. Drawing a long, calming breath, he cast a look over his wing and squinted. He could still see the spires of the aerie, but doubted the sentries could see him. In the distance, he saw a gryfon flying, but in the deceptive evening light, couldn't tell if it flew toward him, or away.

After resting a moment, Stigr forced himself to stand, to move, to feel the pain and walk on anyway. He ducked his head like a wolf, and followed the rabbit trail. The light dimmed, and the damp earth grew steadily colder around him. The trail meandered from brushy spot to sheltering rocks, but Stigr was patient, and didn't mind hunting in the dark, if it came to that.

The wind shifted, and Stigr smelled not rabbit, but something else.

Something far more dangerous. His skin prickled, and he lurched to a stop, staring around. Too late, he remembered Rok's casual observation of possible lions in their territory, but none of the day sentries had mentioned them, so clearly the big cats were testing the boundaries at night.

Stupid, stupid . . .

He could continue on and investigate himself—but not even he was stupid or stubborn enough for that. Friendly lions would not trespass, and he did not want to meet unfriendly lions in the dark—flightless, and alone.

Stigr turned to begin the long trek back to the Dawn Spire, and came face-to-face with Rok, landing hard in front of him. The gryfon he'd seen, flying . . .

"Rok," he muttered, half accusation, half embarrassing relief. His fellow sentry looked refreshed and alert, and was the best thing Stigr had seen all evening. "Valdis sent you."

"She didn't have to," Rok said, his tone breezy, but eyes flicking about toward the shadows. If there were lions, they hid themselves well in the scattered rocks, brush, and the beginning of the sweep of long grass several leaps windward. "She said you went hunting."

"So you followed me."

"I'd rather have accompanied you, if only you'd asked me." Rok's gaze settled on Stigr at last, and in the twilight Stigr saw a myriad of things in his friend's face—deep fondness, frustration, worry. Baldr had given him such looks, once. He'd feared Stigr's stubbornness and recklessness might land him in trouble one day.

Of course, in the end, it was Stigr who had failed to protect his wingbrother.

Rok stepped toward him, extending a wing. "No one should hunt alone, especially not in the dark."

"Especially not me, is that it?"

"Yes," Rok snapped at last, folding his wing and stepping back. "Especially not you. Like it or not, brother, you can't fly. I respect you as a warrior and an equal, but no sane gryfon wanders alone with rogue lions about. Not when he's got no one to fight with him, and no way to escape if he's outnumbered."

Stigr snarled, anger flashing up his chest. He almost sprang at Rok, but deep in his core, Stigr knew his friend was not the source of his trouble. He spoke the truth. He spoke the wretched, agonizing truth, as friend would, as a brother. And for a moment, Stigr hated him.

"Let me help you," Rok said. "Just let me come with you. No gryfon, part of a pride, should have to do things alone. You've spent enough time in this life alone."

A noise drew Stigr's ear back. The scent of lions grew overwhelming.

He turned from Rok's angry, earnest face to blare a warning shriek at the waving grasses behind them. "Show yourselves! You foolish cubs are upwind, and I know you're there."

Rok strode up on Stigr's left. "We're personal friends to Chief Mbari of the First

Plains, and you're trespassing. Explain yourselves and be gone, or I guarantee you'll suffer for it."

In the dying light, six male lions rose around them. Three from the high grass, two from under sheltering slabs of rock, one from the brush.

They were surrounded.

"Tyr's left talon," Stigr muttered. He raised his head, trying to look more impressive than he knew he must. His shoulders and hind legs needled with aches and threatened to betray him. "You stand on gryfon territory. We are friendly if you are. Chief Mbari—"

"We do not answer to Mbari," growled the largest of them. His wildfire mane stood out with feathers—eagle and gryfon, making him look larger, but slightly off balance, as they were arranged with none of the artistry and grace of the lions Stigr knew.

"Figures," Rok said, with a sigh. His tail lashed, switching Stigr across the backs of his hind legs. Stigr managed not to flinch, but the breath nearly left him when his bruise flared.

The leading lion, nearly a rival to the great Mbari in size, if not years, lumbered forward. "Not all of us enjoy licking the tail feathers of gryfons as much as Mbari does. His days as chief are setting, and soon my time will dawn."

"And you are?" Stigr asked incredulously.

Amber eyes flared and the great lion hissed, baring his magnificent teeth. "I am Baako, the Strongest. My brothers and I will have the First Plains, and do away with these gryfon claims on our hunting grounds."

Stigr growled, stepping forward. "Maybe you will, but in the meantime, you're on our land. This seems a matter for Mbari, not us. You should be on your way."

Rok lashed his tail feathers across Stigr's hind legs again, as if trying to force him to sit down. "Forgive my friend. His lameness gives him ill-temper. We understand your grievance, but have mercy and let us leave in peace."

Stigr cast Rok a sharp look, but Rok only gave him an overly piteous glance, and at last Stigr understood. He sank down as if far more exhausted than he was. It stung his pride, but it was better than dying. He was too old to value his pride overly much. "Surely such great warriors as you don't need to bother with an old, wingless gryfon and a single sentry."

"Baako," hissed one of the smaller males from the grass. "You promised me feathers for my mane. I would like his black feathers for my mane, as no other lion has such feathers—"

"Silence," Baako said, turning to pace a circuit around Rok and Stigr. "Why would you seek the feathers of a lame gryfon? You might as well pull a nestling and pluck its feathers for the tuft on your tail. Look, he wears a flower, perhaps to mark his weakness."

Stigr had forgotten the mudding flower. Rok growled at the mention of violence to nestlings, and Stigr's façade of weariness crumbled. He surged to his feet, flaring his wing. "Come at me, *cub*. You will not find my feathers easily won, nor my flower a mark of weakness."

Tyr made you so strong . . .

"Ha," breathed the lion from the grass, and shot forward. With his movement, the rest of the lions leaped from their hiding places and toward the two gryfons.

Rok leaped between them "Idiot—"

"Move!" Stigr shouted. He zig-zagged around Rok and hopped up high, letting the lion run right under him. He dropped to the lion's back and raked his talons along his muscled flank. "You'll have trouble decorating your mane if I shave it from your neck!"

The lion screamed in feline fury and whipped around in a circle in an attempt to throw Stigr from his back. Stigr dug in with talons and hind claws and clamped down on a beak-full of ragged mane.

Baako the Strongest laughed, a surprisingly high, fluting sound, and padded away, apparently content to watch. In the corner of his thrashing vision, Stigr saw Rok, valiantly fending off three lions and attempting to lure them off by alternating between fighting, and flying in short bursts over their heads.

Stigr's opponent dropped to the ground, but before he could roll and crush him, Stigr released his grip and sprang away. His already bruised muscles screamed in protest. He staggered back to catch a breath, and felt fire on his hind quarters. A second lion had darted in, claws lashing. Stigr flashed around, springing up and slashing his talons at the same time. He caught the beast's eye, and was satisfied with his cutting yowl of pain and hasty retreat.

The first attacker slammed into him again and wicked claws lashed Stigr's scarred shoulder, his ribs, his belly. Stigr flailed, twisting his head to try and see his opponent's next movement, only to see yawning jaws lined with long fangs. Yellow teeth snapped shut a feather-breadth from his remaining eye. Stigr shoved his talons up and swiped them down the lion's face.

A snarling yowl told him he'd scored, and the lion grasped him by the shoulders and rolled again, slamming Stigr's back and wing against the damp, hard earth, straddling him.

Stigr thrashed and squirmed his hind legs between himself and the lion and shoved, hard, against his soft belly. The lion coughed but didn't budge, and Stigr managed to clamp his talons on the soft, furry throat. He didn't tear, but he squeezed.

"Yield and leave our lands," Stigr gasped, fighting to get the words out around his throbbing muscles. Rather than try to escape the grip, the lion sank his weight against Stigr's hind claws, then his chest, pressing, using his weight to crush down on him, squeezing the breath from Stigr's chest.

"I'll have your black feathers for my mane," the lion rasped against his talons, and Stigr smelled his blood. "You fought well. You surprised Baako, I think."

Sudden pressure on his own throat was a huge lion paw. Stigr hated to kill, but he tightened his own grip at the lion's throat—but the great cat pressed down, and Stigr couldn't catch a breath. His muscles felt slack. His talons on the lion's throat loosened.

The lion perked his ears, tilting his head.

"End it. . ." Stigr gagged, gasping for air, but rather than a swift, honorable kill, the lion seemed curious to watch him suffocate. His paw pressed harder, and Stigr's vision narrowed to a pinpoint of twilight, then fell black. A soft voice lilted in his ears.

Tyr made you so strong . . .

He remembered the Silver Isles. He saw a bright shore, but it was not the shore of his homeland. Golden light from a sun that never set poured around him, and he heard achingly familiar laughter. Baldr. He had both wings, and all his pain had left him.

All his pain had left him.

But pain is . . . is . . .

"You've done more than I could have hoped," said his dead wingbrother from somewhere Stigr couldn't perceive. *"You can rest now. "*

Stigr reveled in immortal wings, in the strength of having no pain.

"Tyr made you strong," Baldr said, and Stigr almost saw him, almost, in the endless light. *"But you can rest now."*

But he was no longer living for Baldr's memory, nor for Shard . . .

Or for anyone but himself.

The desperate shriek of another, living gryfon cut through Stigr's haze. Rok.

Baldr didn't need him anymore, but another gryfon did.

"Come rest . . . "

"Not yet," Stigr roared. He turned from his wingbrother and the Sunlit Land and dove, dove—and blazed to consciousness, back in the chilly, damp desert of the Winderost, back to one wing, back to a body wracked with pain.

A body wracked with life.

Filled with righteous fury, Stigr slammed his talons against the shocked lion's muzzle, raking down the pale cheeks to give him a scar that would make him wary of gryfons for the rest of his life.

The lion yowled and spit and staggered back, shaking his head and cursing. Stigr whirled, wing flaring. It was almost full dark now. He could barely see, but he heard Rok in distress, saw Baako the Strongest knock him to the ground.

Stigr leaped and landed on the lion's back and slapped him the face with his wing, slashing feathers across his eyes as he dug talons into the tawny pelt. His breath and strength were nearly gone, but he would fight for Rok, would fight for his own life, would teach these lions a lesson they would not soon forget.

"Rok, fly!"

"Will not . . ." Rok crawled to his feet, flaring his wings and ramping up to challenge the two remaining lions who still had the stomach to fight.

"You will!"

"When you're done over there, come and make me!" Rok's wit dissolved to a growl as another lion jumped for him.

"Off me, wretch!" Baako whirled and ramped, and still Stigr held fast. "You're nothing but a wingless, sightless—"

"I am Stigr, son-of-Ragr, warrior of the Dawn Spire, wyrm-slayer, and you will leave my lands!"

"Ha—!" Baako jerked around, bucked hard, and Stigr lost his grip.

The lion flung him to the ground and leaped, bearing over him.

Claws came at his throat and Stigr wondered if he'd flown free of the Sunlit Land only to go right back—when gryfon roars and screams fell down on them, followed by ten strapping members of the King's Guard, led by Asvander himself.

Baako's brothers didn't have the heart for that fight, and fled into the grass and the dark.

"After them!" barked Asvander, landing in a hard lope. "See they make it to the border, and stay there."

Eight of the guard broke off, harrying the lions through the dark. Asvander and the other sentry, Stigr knew it was Valdis' brother Mar by his scent, stalked toward Baako.

The lion shoved off of Stigr, but hesitated. "You will regret this day, when we—"

Rok jumped forward and slapped the lion across the rump with his talons. Baako hissed, spooked, and spun to face the lanky sentry. "Off you go," Rok growled, raising his talons again.

"Leave our lands, or face death," Asvander said coolly. Stigr scraped himself off the ground and stood on wobbly but unbroken limbs, also staring down the lion, for what his stare was worth.

At last, Baako bared his fangs in a final hiss, turned tail, and bounded into the dark.

"After him," Asvander rumbled to Mar.

"A pleasure," growled the old sentry, and jumped into the air. Stigr watched him with a pang of envy, then felt a warm wing press to him.

"All one piece?" Rok peered around, ears perked, as if expecting to see bits of Stigr scattered around the ground. There were quite a few feathers, but that was all.

"Just about. You?"

"Still flying," Rok said. "And now with another good tale for the fires."

"I'm taking all these," Stigr said, hobbling to gather what feathers he could find in the dark. He didn't want scavenging lions claiming any of them.

"Every one," Rok agreed. "You can disperse them among your young admirers."

Stigr snorted.

Rok picked up a single tail feather, ever helpful, and turned to Asvander. "You've got excellent timing, First Sentinel." He mantled halfway to Asvander, who clicked his beak in irritation.

"You're lucky we saw you flying off on your own at all. You might've warned me, or at least said where you were going." He rounded on Stigr. "What were you trying to prove, hunting lions?"

"I was actually hunting rabbits," Stigr mumbled, and found his tongue dry and gummy, as disturbing, quivering waves of weakness trembled up his legs. Hungry, injured, exhausted. That summed him up, but he tried to stand tall and straight in front of the First Sentinel, a pile of his own feathers at his feet.

"I honestly can't say I didn't know this would happen," Rok said, and Stigr found himself unable to process the words, and wondered if Rok meant it that way. "Although Stigr might've. That Vanir gift for prophecy, and all—"

"Be still," Asvander said wearily, and Rok obeyed, though Stigr knew it was only because Asvander would back up the order with talons, if necessary. "We'll stay here tonight, and get you back to the healer tomorrow, Stigr."

"What about me?" Rok asked. "I need a healer too."

"What you need is more duties to fill your time," Asvander said.

Stigr shook his head, trying to clear some dizziness. "I can walk . . ." but the thought of walking back to the aerie buckled him at every joint and he felt to the dirt with a huff, and a groan.

"There we go," Rok said, too cheerily, and plopped down beside him. "It's decided."

Stigr found himself grateful for his friend's warmth. Then, knowing Asvander was keeping a watch for stray lions, he let himself rest at last.

They left in grumpy silence at first light, and it was middlemark by the time they returned to the Dawn Spire. Valdis met them near the stream, as Stigr was hobbling toward the healer and snapping at Rok to keep his distance.

"What in Tyr's bright sky?" Alviss exclaimed.

"Lions," Stigr grunted, glancing around to see the young gryfess from the previous day staring at him with her beak open. "Thanks. Your flower gave me luck." He eyed Rok sideways, and the brown sentry lifted his beak higher. Stigr thought he saw the sentry slide a single black feather over toward the apprentice, but he wasn't sure, and he didn't see the feather later.

"Well stop staring and get to work," Alviss said to the apprentice, and she did.

A young sentry found them as the healers fussed and tended their cuts and bruises.

"When you're finished here, the king would like a word, Stigr."

He wondered why his momentary lapse in judgment warranted an audience with the king, when it was Asvander's place, as First Sentinel, to see to him. Stigr pushed to his feet. "I'll go now—"

"When you're finished here," said the sentry firmly. "The king was very specific that you be treated for your wounds."

"Good because I didn't want to hold him down," Rok said, fluffing his wings.

"As if you could," Stigr snipped, and sat.

They bantered while the healers worked, then left, together, to meet the king.

"Asvander has explained to me that you weren't intentionally seeking lions."

Kjorn lounged with easy majesty along a lower tier inside the crescent of the Dawn Spire itself, holding informal court. Stigr sat before him, too weary to stand and not proud enough to hide it at the moment. Beside the king, who shone gold in the late afternoon sun that graced the Spire, sat Thyra, daugher-of-Caj.

Daughter of Sigrun, Stigr thought, eyeing the lovely queen, and finding a disconcerting resemblance to his old love in her fierce face and brown eyes. She inclined her head to him a fraction.

He returned his gaze to Kjorn. "That's right."

"Yet you knew they might be about, and you left the aerie without any other gryfons to hunt with you?"

"I had Rok with me."

Kjorn ground his beak, looking to Rok, who nodded once. Neither of them mentioned that Rok had joined late, that Stigr had left without him.

"Stigr . . ." The king trailed off, studying him with unmasked consternation. Finally, he chose bluntness. "You are a valuable member of my pride, and from what I see, your current duties no longer suit your needs or skills. I believe it's time for your service in the Guard to come to an end."

That gave Stigr the strength to stand. "Your Highness—"

"This isn't a discussion," Kjorn said. He lifted a wing, as if to reach out and soothe Stigr's temper. "And this has little to do with your capabilities. But you strain yourself to breaking for the Guard when I believe there are places where you might be less frustrated, and more useful."

"Such as?" Stigr growled. "You mean to say I'm not useful in the Guard?"

He looked to Rok, but his friend remained silent, and studied the opposite rock wall with fascination. *Why aren't you backing me up?* Stigr wanted to scream at him.

But Thyra spoke, and Stigr heard Sigrun in her voice, and that silenced him for a moment. "I've just spoken with elder Kesvar, who tells me—"

"I will not join the elder circle. Your Majesties..."

The queen continued as if he hadn't interrupted. "... who tells me that Master Lenvir tires of his duties and wishes to join the elders, himself."

Stigr paused, glancing from Rok's stupidly amused expression, back to the queen. "Lenvir. Isn't he the—"

"Yes," said Thyra, eyes shining with mischief. "He is."

Kjorn stood and stretched, at ease. "This would, of course, mean that we need a warrior to replace Lenvir in his current position. Someone with some experience, who also holds the respect of the pride. Someone, I dare say, with a bit of a frightening reputation."

Stigr looked between them suspiciously.

"They mean you," Rok supplied helpfully, and Stigr cuffed his head.

"If this is because of my wing..."

Kjorn's gaze grew cool, and he stood, and he was as large and imposing as Stigr remembered. "I would not trust the future of this pride to a gryfon I thought anything less than capable. I believe you have much to offer in Lenvir's place, and that is why I'm asking you."

Thyra stood as well, lifting her pale lavender wings. "We would be glad, honored, if you would say yes."

Stigr looked at his monarchs, then found himself looking at Rok, who gave the slightest nod of encouragement. Faced with all of them, and thinking of what Valdis might say later if he refused such an honor, Stigr could only bend his sore muscles and mantle low, spreading his single wing.

"Then I accept. When will I begin?"

"As soon as you're healed," Kjorn said, in a way that brooked no argument. He opened his beak in an amused expression. "You'll need your strength. In the meantime, seek out Lenvir and see what guidance he can offer."

"Yes, your Highness."

He and Rok bowed again, and left the Spire.

"I should check in with Asvander," Rok said, pausing. Stigr stopped beside him, noticing the number of fledges gathered around the stream. There seemed to be suddenly more of them than he remembered.

"See you at supper?" Stigr said, looking over at Rok.

Rok nodded once, and turned to go.

"Rok."

He stopped and turned at once, ears perking, a sudden, hopeful glimmer in his face. Stigr ruffled his feathers. "Thank you. For finding me last night."

One brown ear flicked, and Rok ducked his head. "Of course. Stigr—"

"See you at supper."

Both ears laid back, then Rok gave a forced chuckle and nodded, bounding away to take flight down the canyon.

It was a full turn of the moon before Stigr felt truly ready to begin his new duties. In the meantime, he worked with Lenvir and rested, as ordered by the king, and apologized to Valdis for getting beat up by lions without her.

The first day in his new position dawned golden, though a hint of autumn chill touched the air. Stigr looked forward to the change of seasons. And, he found himself strangely looking forward to *not* climbing the Wind Spire, or struggling to keep pace with the other sentries.

He found himself looking forward most to his new task.

And here they came.

Stigr had chosen new ground just outside the rock formations that formed the aerie, a nice flat expanse rounded by sagebrush on all sides. The dirt was soft and sandy, which would make for some good cushioning, and they were in sight of the sentries, so they would be safe and yet feel the pressure of an audience.

The fledges arrived in groups and one by one, some trying to fly, some loping from trails leading out of the aerie, and lined up before him with giddy eagerness. They tried to look respectful, Stigr thought, but he was apparently something new and exciting, and they whispered and fluffed anxiously among themselves.

"It's going to be hard to hear me if you don't shut your own beaks," Stigr said. The sound of twenty beaks clicking closed ended in obedient silence.

"I am Stigr, son-of-Ragr—"

One flared his short wings. "Is it true you slew a wyrm without even touching it?"

"You flew from the Silver Isles?"

"Is it true you bested six lions last moon? *In the dark?*"

"Did you really challenge Lofgar of the Ostral Shore?"

"Did you once beat First Sentinel Asvander in a spar?"

Impatience and surprise silenced him a moment, then he snapped his beak and lashed his tail. They fell quiet.

He spoke to the fledge nearest him. "You there, what's your name?"

The young male blinked at him in surprise, and Stigr knew why. He also knew his name. There was no other gryfon who bore similar coloring—scarlet face feathers that faded into gold like a sunrise down his back, and eyes of pale summer blue.

There was not a gryfon in the aerie who didn't know this fledge's name, and Stigr had stupefied him by asking.

"I . . . ah . . ."

Somewhere, a young gryfess chittered a giggle.

"Speak up," Stigr said. "Strange, I know, but you'll one day meet a creature who doesn't know you, and it's rude not to introduce yourself."

The fledge puffed up, eyes narrowing, expression sober. "I am Kvasir, son-of-Kjorn, Battle Born, Prince of the—"

"That'll do," Stigr said. "Do you judge others by the stories you hear, Prince Kvasir, or by what you see before you?"

The prince cocked his head, and Stigr was pleased to see him think about the question. "A little of both, Training Master Stigr."

"That's an honest answer."

"Training Master," Kvasir began somberly, "my father says you will also teach us of the Vanir?"

Stigr's chest warmed and he nodded, once. This was Sigrun's grandson. Many of these fledges had ties to the Silver Isles, and he could teach them what they otherwise might never learn. "Yes, I will." Another excited chitter rippled through the group.

"You," Stigr said to a giggling gryfess. She froze and stood tall, angling her head. She was another quarter blood, with striking jade feathers on her head that blended into pale violet-gray wings. "You'd rather serve in the Guard than be a huntress?"

"Yes."

"Yes, what?" Stigr asked.

Her green ears flicked. "Yes, Training Master. I would rather serve in the guard, like my father."

"And you are?"

"Halla, daughter-of-Halvden."

Stigr gave her a second look, and nodded once. "I see you staring at my scar. Do you think having one wing makes me weaker?"

"No, Training Master." Her quiet voice carried over the now-silent, attentive group. "My father says surviving terrible wounds makes us stronger than never suffering wounds at all."

"Well." Stigr flicked his tail. "He would know." He paced down the line of eager warriors-to-be, and raised his voice. "I will teach you all I know about fighting. I will teach you how to defeat a winged foe, and a wingless one. I'll teach you how other creatures fight, and you will heed me, because they have wisdom and cleverness you've never thought of, and you'll surprise your own opponents with new things."

He turned at the end of the line and walked back the other way. Young heads swiveled to follow him. The sun crept over the horizon, painting his new charges in pale golden light. "There are a lot of stories about me. If you work your hardest today and manage to keep your heads out of your tails, I might tell you which ones are true."

This time, they remained quiet, and Stigr nodded his approval.

"Let's begin." He rolled his shoulders, and glanced to the lightening sky. "I want you to imagine a sparrow . . ."

Rok found him at the end of the day, sprawled in the last of the sunlight. "How goes it?"

"Climbing the Wind Spire was easier," Stigr mumbled against the dirt. Exhausted, but utterly satisfied with his day, he rolled to his feet. He was not nearly as tired as his trainees.

Rok watched him stand. "Mbari's last meeting with the king went well. I thought you'd like to know. He's taken matters over, but he's happy to hear we walloped on his rebels a bit. They've gone to ground since."

Stigr chuckled, and found himself oddly relieved to be out of the Guard, but grateful to Rok for keeping him up on the news.

"Supper?" Rok offered, and Stigr nodded with a glance at the last rays of sun. Rok fluffed his feathers and turned to go.

"Rok." Stigr remained where he was, in the dying sunlight. Important things were best done in Tyr's light. "I've thought about things."

"Oh yea?" Rok turned, but this time he was guarded.

"I have an answer for you."

Rok perked his ears, wings lifting a little. "A true one, I hope, and why you waited so long."

Stigr shrugged his wing. The day had filled him with purpose, with confidence, and lightness he hadn't felt since he'd had two wings. "I kept telling myself a lot of things—I was too old, too lame, too content being alone. But none of it's true, and it all came down to fear of failing again."

Rok's gaze hardened and he stepped forward. "You didn't fail Baldr. You did all a wingbrother could ever do. I'll never find a finer gryfon than you, Stigr, nor ask another for this privilege. I'd rather be alone. If you don't want to, say so, but make it 'no,' and not more flying around the question without answering."

Stigr nodded, once.

Then, in the last light of the Winderost sun, he extended his only wing toward Rok.

"Wind under me when the air is still."

Rok's face brightened and he stretched his wing to cover Stigr's. "Wind over me when I fly too high."

"Brother by choice."

"Brother by vow."

"By my—" *wings* . . . Stigr faltered, but Rok continued with stopping.

"While I breathe," he said, "you will never be alone."

"While I breathe," Stigr echoed, finding his voice again, "you will never be alone."

They stared at each other a moment, then Stigr forced a laugh from his tight chest. "You planned that. How long did it take to come up with those words?"

"Not long, really. I had to have something ready in case you managed to get your head straight and accept."

"Fair enough. Maybe now you'll heed my advice on Nilsine."

"Maybe," Rok said cheerfully.

Stigr folded his wing, but Rok left his draped companionably over Stigr's back, and he found he didn't mind. "Let's find Valdis and supper, I'm starved."

"Yes, Training Master." His piping mimic was disconcertingly similar to the fledges Stigr had chased all day.

"Stop it."

"Nooo, Training Master."

Stigr snapped at his wing. Rok lunged forward, and Stigr beat him in a race back to the aerie, where the fires were lit and somewhere, a gryfon was singing tales.

-OoO-

The Salmon Run
A Tale of the Silver Isles

Jess E. Owen

W<small>ATER SLUICED IN A SILVER</small> curtain across the entrance to Shard's den. An overhanging ledge and the sloping rock floor ensured the torrent didn't run into the den, but continued in a splashing waterfall down the entire face of nesting cliffs to the beach.

If a gryfon turned his ears just right, he might hear the mutterings of the entire pride under the seemingly endless rain.

"You might as well stop pacing," Brynja called from the nest. Shard paused, peering out at the rain, then at his mate, whose feathers looked dark russet against the gloom. She flicked her ears forward, watching him as she dangled a frond of sea grass in front of their nestling daughter. "What will you do, fly up and stop the rain?"

"No." Fondness for his family and frustration at the weather flicked about Shard's mind, then he lashed his tail to clear it. "But we must go on with the fishing, or we'll lose the whole run. This rain promises a heavy winter later, and I won't have hungry mouths, when we have so many to feed."

Brynja nodded once, eyeing the rain. "I know it. Will you take the fire stones? In case of snow in the mountains?" In her distraction, she lowered the frond a feather's breadth.

Little Embra, sensing an opportunity, leaped high and swiped the grass from her mother's talons. "Ha!"

Shard laughed, pride swelling to see his daughter's small wings stretch, though they were no good for flying, yet. She clamped the grass in her beak and tumbled out of the nest, romping over to drop the grass at Shard's talons.

"Da, I got a salmon." She mantled low, spreading her small wings. "For the pride."

Shard dropped to his belly and slid the grass frond close, nodding solemnly to his daughter. "Very well done."

She sat up, blinking large eyes in color somewhere between his and Brynja's, a cool amber like a wolf's eyes. "May I join the fishing?"

A soft sound from the nest was Brynja stifling a chuckle, for Embra's tone was so formal, so practiced. Shard wondered how long she'd been waiting to ask. He stretched forward to nuzzle her ears—which she had yet to grow into, large and feathery gray.

"Not this year. Every gryfon who fishes must be able to fly. That is the rule, and the only safe way."

Her façade of formality and control burst into a long yowl of disappointment, and she shot up to all fours to sprint an impatient circuit around their spacious den. "But Eyvindr is going! And he's barely older! I take care of myself. And I could catch a salmon! I'll die of boredom here! And I *want* to—"

"Stop it at once." Shard stood up, lifting his wings, and snapped his beak to gain her attention. Embra rolled to a sulking stop nearer to the nest. Brynja remained where she was, watching calmly from the nest. Since the appeal had been to Shard, she appeared happy to let him handle the tantrum. "Eyvindr is a full year older than you, and he is already flying—"

"Barely," Embra muttered. Shard ground his beak against a sharp response. He understood her eagerness and hated to stifle her, but he couldn't make exceptions for his own daughter when other nestlings would be just as excited and impatient to go. With the rain already a potential problem, looking after curious, flightless kits would be impossible.

"Embra," Brynja said from the nest, "your father has decided, and it's final. Have some dignity."

Embra's ears flattened and she looked briefly to the curtain of rain, then Brynja, and finally Shard. She met his gaze squarely, every feather defiant.

"Tyrant."

A surprised chill touched Shard's heart. Unconsciously, his talons tightened against the rock and he stood silent in surprise. Apparently satisfied with that, Embra marched back up the rock platform to climb into the nest, where she curled into fluffy gray ball as far from her mother as she could manage.

Brynja and Shard exchanged a look and her ears slipped back in uncertainty.

"Where did you hear that word?" Shard asked quietly, at last.

Embra's amber gaze flicked between them and, with sudden awareness of trouble, she fluffed her wings in a shrug. "Just stories."

"Whose stories?" Brynja shifted, leaning over to comb soft talons over Embra's short tail. She tucked her tail away and mumbled something vague.

With grudging admiration, Shard realized Embra was protecting someone. He had a good idea who, but didn't want to drag it out of her. Instead of pressing the point, Shard walked forward and ramped up to set his talons on the nest near Embra's head.

"Embra," he said quietly, and she turned her ears his way. "You will be queen one day. The other kits look to your example and when you are grown, the rest of the pride will as well. All we do is for the good of the pride. I'm *glad* you feel brave enough to go on the run, but I ask that you stay, for the good of all."

For a moment, Embra stared at the white goose down lining the corner of the nest. Then, with a grand sigh, she looked at him once more, and nodded. "Yes, Father. I'm sorry."

She averted her gaze and Shard's hackles pricked up at her continued formality, as he sensed she might be only placating him.

Still, under the watchful eye of Brynja, Ragna, and others, she couldn't get in all that much trouble . . . Shard nipped her ear fondly, felt Brynja's relief emanating from the other side of the nest, and was about to answer when wing beats and voices drew his attention to the entry. Three gryfons landed and stepped in out of the rain, shook their feathers, and mantled low.

Dagr, tall and lean with a metallic copper sheen to his feathers, lead the trio, followed by Tollak, mottle-gray and lavender with a striking falcon's dark mask, and Astri, starlight white against the dreary autumn clouds.

"Tollak!" Embra cried from the nest. "Save me! I'm prisoner in my own nest."

The young warrior laughed and raised his wings in greeting. Embra was beloved of all the pride, but Tollak, who especially loved to teach nestlings fighting and flying, could usually be counted on to assist her in any mischief she might devise. He eyed Shard, who merely lifted his beak in warning, then ducked his head toward Embra. "Next year, little ember. The king has spoken."

She drooped back into the nest, her last hope dashed.

"Your Highness—" Dagr and Astri said at the same time, then stopped, looking at each other.

"We're still going," Shard said, answering the question Dagr would've asked. "We leave today. All fledges capable of ascension and glide. All warrior males. All huntresses who wish to go. We'll need enough talons handy to bear the fish to the shore for salting, and enough to stay and fish the run, and watch for cats."

"Your Highness," Astri said again. "Please. You know what I ask."

Shard struggled against pity and impatience, which blended together as a tight discomfort in his chest. "Astri. He cannot stay in the nest forever."

"Hear, hear," Dagr rumbled heartily. "Little sister, he already jumps at his own shadow and refuses to explore with the others. How long will you—"

"Is there a limit to how long I may grieve?" the white gryfess snarled. "Do you not miss your own brother? The brother you abandoned?"

Dagr's hackle rose slowly, then flattened, and he lowered his head to meet the little gryfess's eyes squarely. "I will not dishonor Einarr's courage by raising his son as a cowar—"

"He is *my* son," Astri growled. "Not yours. And not yours," she turned a blazing look to Shard, then Brynja. Her expression flickered slightly with regret when she spied Embra, eyes huge and staring over the edge of the nest. "The run is dangerous enough without predators, and with this flooding rain, but the mountain cats have been coming lower. Because you," she narrowed her eyes at Shard, "will not enforce our claims on the Sun Isle.

At least with a tyrant king, we had no other predators hunting our plains and woods."

Shard stared at her.

"Astri," Dagr said, voice low and warning.

Shard stepped forward, forcing his ears to remain forward. "They have not encroached our claims. They remain on their own hunting grounds."

"Except when they don't," Astri said, white tail whipping back and forth like skyfire. "What of the rabbits found scattered on *our* land—not eaten, just ripped and scattered. For sport? As a warning? Mocking you? I will not let my son into cat territory as long as this is happening."

Tollak spoke up hesitantly. "We have no proof the rabbits were left by mountain cats."

"Except scent," Astri said. "As plain as—"

"Astri." Shard raised his wings, but dipped his head low to her. "We all grieve Einarr. And no, there is no limit on your grief—or anyone's. He will always be missed. He was my friend. I will always regret his death. But he is gone.

We burn rowan in his memory every year . . . when we should let him go." She lifted fierce eyes to meet his, but remained silent, watching his face. After a moment she looked down, and Shard continued firmly.

"Einarr's courage is his legacy. If you keep Eyvindr always under your wing, he will never have a chance to meet his own destiny, to find his own bravery and honor. Astri, you can't protect him forever. If you try, it will be to his ruin. Let him go."

"We'll take care of him," Dagr said, stretching a wing over her back. She didn't push him away. Looking encouraged, Dagr added, "I promise you."

Rain fell steadily through a moment of quiet.

Finally, Astri lifted her head higher, the picture of wounded dignity. "It seems I don't have much choice." She met Shard's eyes again. "I bow to your wiser judgment. Thank you for hearing me, your Highness."

"Astri," Shard murmured, as a way of accepting her courtesy, even if the words were cool. She took that as her leave and ducked out from under Dagr's wing, throwing herself back into the pouring rain with hard strokes of her wings.

Heavy silence clouded the gloomy den, broken only by the clattering rain. Not even Embra dared to break it.

"Gather everyone," Shard said, not looking at Dagr or Tollak. "It's past time to leave. Brynja, I will take the firestones in case of snow."

They murmured agreement, bowed to him and to Brynja, and left the den.

"Shard," Brynja said, quietly stern from the nest. "It was the right thing."

Shard stared at the rain. "Was it?"

One word echoed in his head, first in the beating of rain on stone, then in Embra's voice, then Astri's.

Tyrant.

THE SCENT OF WOOD smoke and frost woke Shard, and the laughter of gryfons. He rolled to his belly and peered out from under the sheltering boughs of a pine, toward the river and a world suddenly blazing orange and white. Hoarfrost and ice caked the golden birch, the marigold larch, the evergreen pines and stones and riverbanks.

Some time during the night, the rain had ceased, and a pale silver sky promised a blue day. Shard's breath clouded in front of him, and he stared at the crystalline world.

"Fair winds!" Dagr called from afield, throwing sticks onto a newly crackling fire. Shard was grateful they'd brought dry tinder from the nesting cliffs. "Your Highness, Tyr favors the bold! The river is high from the rain but already my scouts spy red salmon coming upstream."

A thrill leaped like a fish in Shard's breast and he sprang up, trotting out and breathing deeply of the chill air.

He had never enjoyed his autumns so much as when they began fishing the salmon run for the first time last year. Worries of Astri and Embra faded from his mind in the face of happy gryfons. All were eager to begin fishing from the chaotic and bountiful run of salmon making their way to the upper mountain lakes from the sea.

A gryfess his age, rosy gray in color and sleek with a huntress's muscle, dove in to land near him. Behind her, more wobbly, glided Eyvindr and Salvi, another fledge of his year. She landed in an excited heap, but Eyvindr touched down with such hesitant care it made Shard's shoulders flinch. Both fledges were second generation mixed bloods, Aesir and Vanir, with bold and startling colors—Salvi, jade green with sapphire flecks along her breast, and Eyvindr, his head and chest star-white like Astri, his wings copper brown like his father and uncle. Both were gangly, mostly limb and wing, like all fledges.

"Keta," Shard said to gryfess who led them, stretching his own wings. "How does it look downriver?"

"Teeming! They'll be on us before middlemark." She laughed, nudging a wing against Salvi. "These two nearly fell into the river after them."

"Did *not*," Salvi said, lifting her head stubbornly.

"I wouldn't on purpose," Eyvindr said, more subdued, and Shard wondered if he had fallen. Still, no special attention. Eyvindr received enough of that in his own nest and had become hesitant and wincing for it. These days on the river would be good for him.

Tell yourself that, Shard berated, *and you'll feel less guilty for ripping a fledge from his mother's side . . .*

"I thought I smelled a mountain cat," Eyvindr said, so softly Shard barely heard him. "Or a fox. And when I looked, I lost my balance. But I didn't fall."

Frustrated with Astri for filling Eyvindr with her shadow fears, Shard shook his head. "That's why we have sentries. There are no cats near. And if there were, we'd see them first."

"Mother says you only see a cat just before it kills you."

Salvi laughed. "You're spooky as a grouse. Wooo . . . look out!" She crouched, about to pounce, but Keta blocked her with a wing.

"Stop. There is nothing dishonorable about watching for danger." Salvi blinked, and sat down obediently. Eyvindr had already fallen to a defensive posture, one Shard recognized as signature to the training of his own nest-father, Caj. At least Astri was allowing him out of the nest to learn how to fight. He looked as if he would say something more, then seemed to read Shard's expression and remained silent.

Shard glanced around for a way to get the fledges out of earshot. He didn't see Tollak, who was usually stuck to Dagr's side. Supposing he must have taken another group of fledges downriver, Shard decided these two could take his place. "You two go help Dagr with the fires. For now, we wait for the salmon."

Eyvindr's gaze brightened at his uncle's name, and Shard was pleased to see him perk up and dash away with some energy to make himself useful. Salvi followed, but made a point of shoving off the ground to fly the short distance instead of run.

Shard stepped closer to Keta, who looked fresh and happy in the cold morning. "How are they doing?"

"Well enough," she said, though her gaze trailed Eyvindr. "He hesitates, and that will make him fall, if he's not careful. But this . . . this will be good for him." She glanced at Shard sidelong, and lowered her voice. "It was the right thing, my lord."

Shard fluffed his feathers. "Does everyone know about our argument?"

"Oh yes," she said simply. "But it was bound to happen sooner or later. Most fledges his age are fighting to get out of the nest, but he . . ."

"He's afraid," Shard said, feeling gloomy despite the growing light and bluebird sky.

Keta didn't answer, and he looked at her, this Vanir huntress who had come out of exile with her mother and shown herself to be a leader in the pride. She supported Shard, she loved Brynja and Embra, and he valued her deeply.

"Or?" he asked quietly, but she kept her thoughts to herself for a moment, thinking.

All around them, gryfons rose and greeted the clear sky with happy exclamations, wandering to the river to peer up and down the banks in anticipation. The more experienced of the huntresses directed others in hauling dead birch trunks into the water to form obstacles and slow the fish.

"I don't think he's afraid," Keta said finally, her voice measured as she scanned the river and the tree line.

"Then?" he pressed.

She looked back at him, thoughtful. "I think he worries about his mother. More than he should. I think he fears that leaving her side would be seen as . . . I don't know, Shard." She dropped into informality, which Shard preferred. "She fears losing him more than anything in the world, and he *knows* that. How can he leave her to do anything when he knows that?"

Struck by her observation, Shard turned to watch Eyvindr again. The whole flight up the canyon the young gryfon had been silent, fretting, flying poorly and full of tension. After an evening beneath the stars, a good night's sleep under his uncle's wing and a morning of freedom, he seemed to be loosening up. He bounded to and fro with growing energy, eager to do as he was told.

"It was just my thought," Keta said softly.

"I think you might be on to something," Shard said. "Still, keep a close eye. He can't be hesitant with the river."

"Trust him," Keta said. "Trust him as Dagr does, give him responsibility. I think he will rise to the occasion."

"I will." Shard sighed, then shook himself. He least of all could show that he worried for Eyvindr, for how would *that* make the young gryfon feel? As tension crawled down his wings he added, "And let's send a patrol downriver. If he did smell a mountain cat, I want it long gone before we spread out and focus on the fishing."

She brightened. "I will. He'll be glad to know you took him seriously."

Shard ducked his head. "I do. I shouldn't have dismissed him so quickly." He drew a long breath, shaking off frustrations. "Tyr has given us a beautiful day. Let us use it."

"Yes, my king!" Keta laughed and sprang away like a fledge herself to pass along his orders for a patrol.

The rest of the morning unfolded into a chilly breeze and blue sky. The frost melted into dampness beneath their talons, and by the time they spied the red waves of salmon thrashing upriver, they were more than ready to fish.

The sunmarks stretched along in happy shouting and chaotic splashing. They lined the fledges along the shallow banks to practice hooking the slower fish inside the birch-trunk corrals, and the red, hook-snouted salmon began to pile up on the banks. They divided some to eat that evening, and more for the carriers to fly back to the nesting cliffs to salt and save for the winter.

Shard checked on each fledge, pleased to see all of them with respectable catches for the day. He paused near Eyvindr, who worked with every gangly limb to drag a fat female salmon from the water.

Seeing Shard, he paused. "Don't worry. We leave every other one to swim and spawn, as you said. But Mother loves the fish eggs so much. I thought someone might take this one back, to show her . . ."

"Keep it," Shard said warmly. "Thank Tor, and keep it, and be proud. You've done very well today."

Eyvindr lifted his beak, every white feather of his neck fluffing with pride. "Thank you, my lord."

Shard nodded once and moved on. He was about to check on Salvi when a long, shrieking call of alarm stopped all of them. Heads turned toward the sky. Brynja, followed by Ragna, Ketil, and Caj, flew in a wedge, fast and straight toward the camp.

There was no reason for them to leave the nesting cliffs. No reason. So the sight of all of them together, flying hard, sent horror down Shard's back.

There was no reason. Unless something was terribly wrong. . .

"Now, Shard," Caj began as he landed, but Brynja rushed forward to meet him first.

"Shard! Oh, Shard . . ." Brynja's feathers stood on end, and before he could ask, she said through hard gasps, "Embra is missing!"

"I didn't do this, my lord." Tollak stared at Shard, who paced in front of him. Starlight gleamed down on them, frosty and distant on top of the King's Rocks. They'd returned to the nesting cliffs, leaving the fishing camp in the care of only a few while the rest searched for the royal nestling.

"I didn't see you all morning, and now she's missing. You know how she wanted to see the salmon. You've helped her disobey me before, all in good rebellion and fun. Before, I forgave it—carrying her on night flights, swimming, hunting the woods—all forgivable." He bore down on the terrified gryfon, his heart cold with fury and fear. All afternoon he'd flown, hunting for his daughter, but there was no sign.

That was the strangest part. No sign.

"But I swear . . ."

He managed not to shout. "Tollak. This is very serious, she could be in danger. Where is she?"

"I—I didn't—this morning, I only, was in the woods. I scented fox, and . . . I—I went to run it off. My king, I didn't take Embra anywhere! The last time I saw her was in your den before we flew upriver, I swear it."

"Shard—my lord," Keta said softly. "He's telling the truth. Look at him."

Shard did. Tollak cowered before him, hunched, wings splayed, head low as if Shard might strike him down. He forced himself to slow his breathing.

The fishing had halted as Shard sent search parties fanning between every bit of land between the fish camp and the nesting cliffs. All along the river, through the mountain pass and the foothills and plains. Every able-bodied gryfon in the pride hunted for Embra all afternoon, but she was nowhere to be found. Brynja led a search now. They took turns, one staying at the rocks in case Embra was found, and one hunting.

Shard fought against mindless anger and accusation. Of course Tollak wouldn't disobey him.

But someone else might.

"Where is Astri?" he demanded.

Tollak sat up straighter. "You can't think . . ."

Shard flattened his ears. "And why not? She was unhappy that I took Eyvindr with us. Maybe she thought to frighten me—"

"She would never," Keta said sharply. "My king, you aren't thinking clearly. No one would purposefully frighten you this way."

Tollak, emboldened by Keta, stood slowly. "You saw how much she wanted to go. Perhaps she—"

"Perhaps she what?" Shard's tail lashed, and he couldn't hold back a snarl. "Perhaps she ran away? Hid from everyone, trying to come up to the salmon run? Covered her own trail so we wouldn't be able to track her . . ."

". . . and got lost?" Keta offered, along the line that Shard had started in irony, but realized was more and more reasonable than one of his own pride kit-napping the princess in order to frighten him.

Of course she hadn't.

No. Astri would not do that.

"But she couldn't possibly get lost," Shard said, feeling deflated. His own daughter had run away and gotten herself in trouble, but his first action was to blame loyal members of his pride. And she had to be in trouble, for if she knew how they searched and worried, she wouldn't stay in hiding. Not even she was so rebellious. "She knows to follow Nightrun if she gets confused in the woods. But that means . . ."

"It means she may be in danger," Keta said quietly. "But not that one of your own took her."

Shard drew a shuddering breath. They were right. He knew they were right. But it didn't calm his fear. "We keep looking—"

"My lord."

The voice from the dark struck his memory like stones ringing together. For a wild moment, Shard thought Einarr spoke to him, as he had once in a dream. But he turned to see Eyvindr climbing the rocks, without a shred of hesitancy, and mantle to him.

"Yes, Eyvindr," Shard greeted numbly.

"I might know where Embra has gone."

Shard perked his ears, surprised at Eyvindr's boldness, grateful, trying to separate him from the image of his dead father and his clinging mother, and treat him as a young warrior of the pride—and his daughter's trusted playmate. "Where? We've searched every speck of ground between here and the fish camp, and found no scent or sign."

"Yes, my lord. I wish I'd thought of it sooner, but it's just come to me . . ." Eyvindr's wings twitched, giving away his nervousness. Shard wondered how harried and frightful he must look, to strike fear into the heart of a fledge who might very well grow to be bigger and stronger than himself one day. "You see, we've searched every speck of ground . . . *above* ground."

Eyvindr met his eyes with pointed surety.

Clarity like starlight pierced through Shard's anger and fear. "Of course," he breathed. "Keta, Tollak—"

But his faithful huntress and warrior had already whipped about and taken flight, calling for others to join them as they flew toward the birch woods, toward the river, toward a slash in the ground that led to a once-secret labyrinth of underground caves.

"Embra!"

"Embra!"

Embra, embra . . . Their shouts echoed through the damp, cold stone.

Ember-rah-em-raa-ra . . .

Shard raced through the caves with Brynja at his heels, not caring if he got himself lost, if they only managed to find Embra again. She wouldn't know their markings, their careful paths through the tunnels that led to other islands. He couldn't let himself despair, or think how long she might've been wandering the caves alone, or shouted for help, growing hungry, and cold . . .

"Embra!"

"When I get my talons on you—" Brynja shouted, "you won't go anywhere until the snow falls!"

"I smell *fox*." Eyvindr's voice bounced down an adjacent tunnel.

"If she followed a fox . . ." Shard breathed, and Brynja snarled, low in her chest.

"I will have its pelt for our nest."

Shard turned down the tunnel Eyvindr had taken. "Eyvindr?"

Pale, softly glowing fungi and lichens sprouted along the tight stone corridors formed by flowing lava in the First Age. It was an eerie place, ancient, silent, and the longer Shard remained underground, the tighter his breath became, as his mind flashed back on a tiny prison of ice and stone that had once held him . . . Shard shook himself. He could leave this tunnel any time he liked. He was not trapped here.

But Embra was, somewhere.

"There was definitely a fox here." Eyvindr brought him around.

"You have the nose of a wolf," Brynja said, lifting her own beak to smell, and looking at a loss.

"I think I smell Embra, too." The fledge stood at a dead end, a blockage of tumbled stone. He turned in a circle, ears flicking back and forth. "Embra!"

A faint whimper met Shard's straining ears. "Quiet."

Brynja and Eyvindr went still. Down other tunnels they heard gryfons calling, and Embra's name echoing in endless desperation across the stone.

Then . . .

"Here!"

"She's right here!" Eyvindr cried, and set his talons to the tumbled stones, pulling them away as he spoke. "I knew it. Fox probably—knew just—what—he-was-doing—"

"Stay there!" Brynja and Shard dug with him, dragging back the larger stones.

Pebbles and rock debris fell toward them until they cleared a space large enough for Eyvindr to crawl through. Without hesitation, he shoved himself through the crack and for five awful heartbeats Shard waited, staring at the dark stones.

Dust and pebbles scattered from the hole and there was Embra, with Eyvindr shoving her through the crack and toward Shard and Brynja.

"Da!" She slid down the rock pile and into Shard and Brynja's huddled, winged embrace.

"How could you," Brynja whispered.

"I . . ." she looked between them. "I was in the woods. I saw a fox, dragging rabbits, and I thought he was . . . I thought he was trying to make us think mountain cats were—so I chased him, and tried to catch him, but he led me down here . . ."

Shard ground his beak. "You're fine. It's all right. Embra. Tell us later. You're all right, and that's all we care about. For now."

More rocks bumped down as Eyvindr pulled himself back out from behind the stone wall, and he tumbled down to rejoin them. Brynja threw herself at him, bumping her head against his wing and wrapping her own wing around him.

"Well done, Eyvindr. Clever fledge. Well done."

"Yes." Shard straightened, regarding him. "Your mother will be proud."

Eyvindr looked at him with fierce eyes.

Shard lifted his beak higher. "And I am, too." He drew a slow breath, letting his muscles relax now that his daughter was close again, and inclined his head to Eyvindr. Now that he'd left the nest and proven himself brave and clever, Shard felt a spark of excitement to think what Einarr's son might become. "Thank you, Eyvindr. Embra, say—"

"Thank you, Eyvindr," she whispered, turning full-moon eyes on her new hero.

Eyvindr managed to mantle under Brynja's wing, then he straightened, somber. "Now about this fox. Let me help hunt it, my lord."

Warring anger and curiosity kept Shard silent a moment. Then he shook his head. "I'll deal with the fox, as I handle disputes with all Named creatures. Embra, do you bear him ill-will?"

"No," she said immediately. "I . . . I hunted him first. And he must be leaving rabbits around for a reason."

"Then he fears to speak to me," Shard said, thinking it through. "Or he is trying to scare mountain cats off his territory by fooling them, and it has nothing to do with us." Shard felt the crawling headache of kingship ease its familiar way up his neck. "I will find him, and handle it either way. For now—"

"For now, back to the nest to sleep," Brynja said, herding Embra with her wing. "And let this be a lesson why we don't wander . . ."

Brynja walked ahead, scolding a meek princess, and Eyvindr fell in just behind Shard in the cramped tunnel. "You have to admit it was brave for her to hunt him at all," the fledge whispered to Shard.

He flicked his tail, and tried not to chuckle. "Yes. Yes, it was, wasn't it?"

Back at the fish camp for the final night of the run, Shard stood near the bank, under the starlight. Behind him, two fires crackled, surrounded by gryfons, and the scent of smoke and some roasting fish made him realize he hadn't yet eaten that day.

Dagr trotted up to him. "A good run, my lord. We'll be well set even if the coast freezes hard."

"Thank you for everything, Dagr, for keeping it going when Embra was lost."

Dagr huffed and flicked his tail. "Of course. What else were we to do? And what of the fox she spoke of?"

Shard shook his head. "Gone. Ketil and Astri have led hunt after hunt, and no sign. Perhaps he fears we'd kill him for leading Embra into a trap."

"I might've," Dagr grumbled, "if I'd caught the pest."

"At least we know that mountain cats aren't in our lands."

"For now," Dagr said, and Shard looked at him sidelong. Dagr shifted his talons in the river gravel. "My lord, Astri was upset when she spoke of them, but she wasn't wrong. If this fox felt the need to try scaring off mountain cats by imitating one and living so close to us, that means they're coming lower. Let me run deeper patrols, and lay stronger markers on our boundaries. We've made peace in the islands, but that doesn't mean we allow others to crawl all over us, wherever they want to hunt. If Embra going missing isn't enough proof—"

"Yes, Dagr." Shard sighed. He wanted to believe that if gryfons were at peace that they had no enemies, no troubles. But there would always be dangers. "I agree with you. But no killing, if we can help it. A stronger show of force should do it."

"Yes, my lord."

For a moment they let the river slip over their feet, and before Dagr could ask him Shard said, "Eyvindr did very well. He's a credit to you."

"And Astri," Dagr said, in his loyal way. "He fears to leave her alone, and she fears to lose him, but that doesn't mean she's done poorly by him. It only means they're family. A good family."

"I know." Shard wanted to be angry at her for stifling one of his young warriors, but his own terror when Embra had gone missing softened his frustration and deepened his understanding of her fears. "I know that."

"I know you do," Dagr said, bumping a wing against him in a brotherly way. "Which is why you are the greatest king these islands have known, or will ever know."

Shard laughed weakly. "You've known only two other kings, and neither were fit to rule."

"Both were tyrants," Dagr agreed, and the word rang unpleasantly. *Tyrant.* Shard looked at him slowly. "Which is why I will always be grateful for you. And why I teach Eyvindr the same."

"What do you teach him?" Shard felt the starlight, distant, watching. "Dagr, Embra said the word tyrant, and I've never spoken it to her."

"I know." Dagr averted his gaze. "But don't you agree it's important to teach them? To teach them the history—Sverin's redemption, yes, but also his fall? If they don't know where we've come from, they may one day end up back there."

Shard couldn't answer that. He tried not to paint his distant wingbrother's father as a villain in his stories to Embra . . . but maybe Dagr was right. Maybe he did her a disservice.

"Only in stillness, the wind," he mused.

Dagr skipped to the end of the song by adding, "It was only by knowing the other, that they came to know themselves. My lord, we must know ourselves by knowing that we came from war. Eyvindr is battle-born, like Halvden's daughter, like Kjorn's son. They were borne of conquering, of war, and came into this world during a *battle*." He turned, talons swishing through the cold water, to face Shard fully.

"Even Embra is Brynja's daughter because you flew to the Winderost seeking answers. Only by knowing all of the story, by knowing the dark, will they also know the light. Yes, I call Sverin a tyrant when the nestlings ask me. I also call him a warrior, *and* a king. We can't hide from own our legacies, my lord, or we'll be ruined by them if the young ones learn we hid any of the truth from them."

Shard closed his eyes. Embra was so young. He thought on Dagr's words, on his legacy. On what kind of pride Embra would inherit.

At length, letting the river cool his talons and his heart, he spoke. "Thank you for being honest with me. I hope you always will. But I don't know if Embra is ready to hear the whole tale, the darkness, and all of it. She's so young."

Dagr watched him, unblinking. "So were you, when your father was slain, and you were put in the nest of your enemy's son."

"Dagr," Shard warned. "Kjorn—"

"Is honorable and just, because he was your friend. Your friendship saved him. It saved all of us. But think how you felt when you learned the truth of the Conquering, and how long it took you to understand that the world was not at all as you'd been raised to believe. Let us be honest with our kits, Shard. Let us at least be honest."

Shard watched him, knowing he was right, but struggling still. He wanted to protect Embra from the darkness—the very thing he condemned Astri for doing to Eyvindr.

"Protect her too much, " Dagr said, "and it will be to her ruin."

Shard closed his eyes at hearing his own words offered back to him. "We'll never really be rid of it, will we? The past?"

"No, of course not. But, I'll tell you what I tell Astri—"

"We have hope," Shard said softly. "I know that's what you say." Dagr ducked his head in agreement. Somewhere upstream a salmon splashed, and Shard ticked an ear toward it. "We have hope, as we've never had before. I have faith in my pride, and in my daughter."

"Good," Dagr said. "Because we all have faith in you—and *that* is what gives us hope and lights our future."

Shard nodded once, running his talons through the river gravel, thinking on the salmon run. The fish, hatched in the cold mountain lakes, took a treacherous journey downstream to live their lives in the sea, only to return, on some ancient call, to the waters where they'd been born. There they spawned and died, letting the next generation be born in cold water, run downstream, and begin again.

And again . . . and again.

It was a hallow thing, the salmon run, and Shard closed his eyes a moment to thank all of them, Named or not, for their lives, and for letting him be a part of their song. A thousand whispers rose and faded in his heart . . . or perhaps he just heard the rushing water, close and distant and unending. The thing that settled in his heart at last was hope, after all, for Embra and the future and all the pride.

Dagr stepped back from him, drawing Shard's thoughts to earth. "And now, my king, may I encourage you to eat something before you end up skinnier than Tollak?"

Shard laughed, and waded out of the water with a shiver, and Dagr followed.

They were met with hearty cheers, and as Shard settled to eat, gryfons reported a final tally of the fish, and they ate until they groaned, and they sang, and they slept at last under the cold and sparkling autumn sky.

-oOo-

Can't get enough gryphons? Support Jess on Patreon for sneak peeks at artwork, flash fiction, writing tips, and more!
www.patreon.com/ authorjessowen

About the Author

JESS HAS BEEN CREATING WORKS of fantasy art and fiction for over a decade. The Summer King Chronicles is her first foray into the publishing realm, and she plans many more gryfon adventures to come. Her short fiction has appeared in Cricket Magazine for young readers, and various anthologies online. She's a proud member of the Society of Children's Book Writers and Illustrators, the Science Fiction and Fantasy Writers of America, and the Authors of the Flathead. Jess lives with her husband and their dog in the mountains of northwest Montana, which offer daily inspiration for creating worlds of wise, wild creatures, magic, and adventure. Jess can be contacted directly through Facebook, Twitter, and her website, www.jessowen.com.

Made in United States
Orlando, FL
28 August 2023

36519133R00121